Lucia led the m

'Is Matthieu a French ...
way?' she asked, then ... ...ave
thought of a more scin... ...nversational
gambit.

'It is, but the English quarter of me insists on
being called Matt by friends and workmates.'

He smiled at her, a warm, conspiratorial smile
that made the skin along her spine prickle with
an awareness she had never felt before.

'And which quarter of you is English?' she asked,
then blushed when she realised that the question
was badly phrased.

Having pursued many careers—from school-teaching to pig farming—with varying degrees of success and plenty of enjoyment, **Meredith Webber** seized on the arrival of a computer in her house as an excuse to turn to what had always been a secert urge—writing. As she had more doctors and nurses in the family than any other professional people, the medical romance seemed the way to go! Meredith lives on the Gold Coast of Queensland, with her husband and teenage son.

Recent titles by the same author:

COURTING DR GROVES
PRACTICE IN THE CLOUDS

WINGS OF DUTY

BY
MEREDITH WEBBER

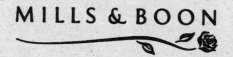

MILLS & BOON

MILLS & BOON, the Rose Device and
LOVE ON CALL are trademarks of the publisher.
Harlequin Mills & Boon Limited,
Eton House, 18-24 Paradise Road, Richmond, Surrey TW9 1SR

© Meredith Webber 1996

ISBN 0 263 79999 9

Set in Times 10 on 12 pt. by
Rowland Phototypesetting Limited
Bury St Edmunds, Suffolk

03-9612-48081

Made and printed in Great Britain

CHAPTER ONE

THE lean, trim young man, in a serviceable blue shirt and stone-washed jeans faded almost to white, was wandering through the tropical plants that turned the base garden into an oasis of green in an otherwise drab suburban desert.

'Are you looking for the visitors' centre? They don't open until. . .'

The words dried on Lucia's lips as the stranger turned to face her, and she found herself looking into the bluest of blue eyes. Not the dark, almost navy blue the writers of her favourite romances seem to love, nor the violet shade that contact lenses could produce. These eyes were the clear blue of the flash on a kingfisher's wings; the sunny blue of the sky in winter. And they were smiling into hers in such a twinkling way that her legs felt shaky.

'No, no!' the man assured her, a shadow of an accent curling the words deliciously into her senses. 'I think I have found what I'm looking for.'

He continued to gaze at her and she felt her cheeks grow warm, while her mind darted off at a tangent. If only she'd worn the new white sun-dress she'd bought last pay-day instead of her old, smart but comfortable yellow shorts and their matching cream and yellow patterned shirt.

The absurd thought startled her back down to earth.

'Well, that's OK, then,' she said awkwardly. 'Enjoy your visit to the Bay.'

She hurried past him, sliding open the doors and escaping into the air-conditioned coolness of the building.

And why had she been so certain that he was a stranger in town? Rainbow Bay was almost a city and she certainly didn't know everyone who lived here.

'Morning, Lucia!'

'Good morning, Mrs Cooper.'

She returned the greeting as she walked towards Leonie Cooper, tucked away in her office behind a door that was labelled BASE MANAGER. Leonie was a friend of her aunt's and it was she who had suggested that Lucia gain some work experience at the Rainbow Bay base of the Royal Flying Doctor Service. Bored and lonely, Lucia had leapt at the chance to do something useful.

Then, three months ago, the base had decided to computerise all their patient files and she had been offered a paid clerical position, her main task being to feed the masses of information into the electronic systems.

'And how's the taste of freedom?' Leonie asked, a smile smoothing the frown lines from between her eyes.

'It's really strange,' Lucia admitted, pausing by Leonie's desk. 'I love living here in town and meeting new people and Aunt Steph is great, but I miss the farm, and the boys and Dad, and I worry about Mum most of the time. . .'

She hesitated, unable to find the words to explain.

'Your mother encouraged you to leave home, Lucia,' Leonie reminded her gently. 'She felt you'd been tied there too long.'

Lucia nodded.

'But I didn't mind, Mrs Cooper,' she said slowly, then shook off the homesickness that seemed to nag at her soul even on the busiest of days. 'Anyway, I love working at the base and the staff are all wonderful to me, even Dr Flint who teases me about—'

For the second time that morning she felt heat rush into her cheeks.

'I'll speak to Dr Flint,' Leonie promised in a voice that made Lucia sorry she'd said anything. 'And I think I can understand why you feel confused. Many families dissolve when tragedy strikes them, but yours grew closer together.' Could it be envy that Lucia heard in the older woman's voice? 'And, although at times you might have felt smothered by that love you miss its warmth and closeness.'

Again Lucia nodded. That was exactly how she felt.

'It doesn't worry me all the time, and I know Mum is receiving the best of care,' she assured her boss. 'It just makes it hard to say I really love everything about being here and the job and all.'

Again she saw the smile flash across the lovely face and, as she picked up the pile of filing that was her first task each morning, she wondered why a woman as attractive as Mrs Cooper hadn't remarried. Had she loved her first husband so much that she could never love another man?

She pulled open the drawer of the filing cabinet and an image of blue eyes appeared in her mind. How silly, she thought, slotting old roster sheets neatly into place. I don't even know what he looked like! All I can remember are his eyes.

'Mrs Cooper?'

And his voice! It took every bit of will-power she possessed not to turn around and stare in amazement at the voice's owner. Mrs Cooper had told her to go on with whatever she was doing if someone came into the office. If there was anything confidential to be discussed she would ask Lucia to make some coffee, which would get her out of the room unobtrusively.

'I'm Matthieu Laurant. Dr Gregory said you'd be expecting me.'

Matthieu Laurant, the new doctor! Lucia remembered the strange spelling on the employment documents she'd filed last week. A Frenchman who had trained at a hospital in England. Her heart felt as if it were expanding in her chest, taking up all the air space until she wondered if she would explode with the urge to turn around and look at him again.

'You could get us coffee, please, Lucia.'

Mrs Cooper's cool, deep voice brushed past her ears but it was several seconds before the words registered.

Turning slowly away from the filing cabinet, she looked again at the man she'd met in the garden. He was smiling at her. Not a wide open sort of smile with teeth showing but a kind of knowing grin, stretching full, pale lips until they tucked dimpled creases into his cheeks.

With his blue eyes and close-cropped brown hair he looked more like a cheeky medical student than a doctor!

'This is Lucia Delano,' Leonie introduced her. 'She's a recent but very valuable addition to our clerical staff.'

Lucia squirmed under the praise in Mrs Cooper's voice. She sometimes wondered if they had manufactured the job for her out of kindness, yet the compliment made her sound like a real member of the team.

'Matthieu is taking James's place,' Mrs Cooper added, disapproval replacing the praise in her now stern tones. James had decided that the erratic work of a Flying Doctor was not the glamorous life he'd supposed it to be and had left suddenly, throwing rosters into chaos.

'How do you do?' the man said, stepping forward and holding out his hand. 'When we met in the garden I didn't realise you were on the staff here.'

Lucia felt his hand grip hers before she realised that she'd held it out.

'Oh, I'm new—I don't— How do you do?'

'Coffee, please, Lucia.'

Her boss saved her from further embarrassment with the reminder and she withdrew her hand from Matthieu's warm clasp and fled, but not before a quick wink from one of those devastating blue eyes had cast her into further confusion.

'Morning, Lucia.' Susan Stone, a nursing sister who had been at the base since it opened fifteen years earlier, was in the small kitchen, tapping her foot as she waited for the water in the urn to boil.

'Good morning, Susan. The new doctor's here.'

'Young and good-looking, is he?'

Susan's teasing response made her realise how rattled she was by the encounter and, for the third time in half an hour, she found herself blushing. She opened the cupboard door and stuck her head inside, pretending to search for the least chipped mugs. Blushing was something she almost never did these days!

'He's got lovely blue eyes,' she heard herself

admitting, but whether to Susan or the coffee-mugs she wasn't certain.

'Life will be fraught with interest,' Susan muttered drily.

'Urn not boiled yet? Thought you were on the clinic flight today, Susan. Good morning, gorgeous!' Peter's voice!

Lucia forgot about chipped edges and pulled two mugs at random from the cupboard. She couldn't let Peter Flint see how she'd reacted to the new doctor. He would *never* stop teasing her about it.

'Good morning, Dr Flint!' she said coolly.

He was the only person at the base, apart from Mrs Cooper, she called by his surname. It was the best way to keep a flirt like him in his place, she'd decided when she'd first met him. And flirt he was! Hadn't she seen with her own eyes the way he carried on with any woman under eighty who came within a radius of one hundred metres of his charming smile and glib tongue?

He acknowledged her greeting, and then Susan was explaining that one of her twins was sick so Christa had offered to do the clinic flight to save Susan and her husband pilot, Eddie, both being away overnight.

'Christa volunteering for a trip to Caltura?' Peter queried. 'I wonder if she might have a man stashed away out there.'

At Caltura—a tiny outpost in the middle of nowhere? The thought diverted Lucia momentarily, then Susan was speaking again.

'Trust you to put a bad connotation on a good deed,' she said sharply. 'Maybe if you stopped chasing every woman in sight, you might find the happiness that seems to elude you so successfully.'

Looking from one to the other, Lucia was surprised to see Peter flinch—as if Susan's words had cut into his skin. And it was the first time she'd heard Susan snap at anyone. Was she more worried than she seemed about her sick child? Or was it simply the humid, sticky heat of early summer making people edgier than usual?

'Urn's boiled,' Peter pointed out, defusing the tension that had suddenly sprung up in the small room. 'Who was first?'

Lucia waved her hand to Susan, who stood back.

'You'd better make the boss's before I fix mine. Coffee might put her in a better mood when I explain that I've left Friday's clinic report on the kitchen table at home.'

Although the base was officially under the control of Jack Gregory, the chief doctor, no one would have argued with Susan's labelling of Leonie Cooper as 'the boss'. With her firm, calm insistence on order and routine she kept a group of diverse and excitable personalities in line, and ensured that the service provided to people in isolated places was the very best that money, time, good organisation and expertise could provide.

As she carried a tray with two mugs of coffee, milk, sugar and a plate of biscuits back into the office, Lucia heard the base manager explaining part of this to Matthieu.

'Our area spreads from here, west across the ranges to cattle properties as big as England. We cover one large mining town, seventeen small mines and prospecting camps, four inhabited islands off the coast and a prawn-trawling fleet that operates north-west of here. We also have all the new adventurers, the ordinary men

and women who have taken off to ''see Australia'' in
family cars or four-wheel-drive vehicles—'

'And off-road bikes!'

Lucia was setting the tray on the desk when Matthieu
interjected, and she looked up enquiringly at him.

'I have just ridden around your vast country on such
a bike,' he explained, to her as much as to Leonie. 'It
was a grand adventure, but I was glad I had an HF radio
with me at all times and knew the network of the Flying
Doctor Service was spread around me when I was many
miles from civilization. It made me feel I had a special
star, up there in the blaze of the night sky, watching
over me.'

'A poet as well as an adventurer,' Leonie suggested,
and Lucia decided that her boss sounded indulgent
rather than disapproving, which was strange. She had
certainly disapproved of James, and was always 'speaking to' Dr Flint about his behaviour.

Leaving the two to enjoy their coffee and finish their
discussion, she headed back to the files. Being an adventurer seemed a totally inconceivable thing to her, but
then she'd reluctantly come to the conclusion that she
was a home body. She'd been nearly twenty-one before
she'd plucked up the courage to leave home and move
to town—a full one hundred and fifty kilometres away!

She crossed to the next filing cabinet and slotted
Eddie Stone's latest flight report in with the other pilot
reports, but her mind was on her own behaviour. Would
she have made even that small move if Anthony hadn't
been so insistent that she make a decision about their
relationship—one way or the other? If his family and
her brothers hadn't been so obvious in wanting an
engagement between them?

Or if her invalid mother hadn't said, 'Go!' and arranged to employ a carer who would see to her personal needs, a job Lucia had done for years with love and tenderness?

'Lucia will give you the guided tour and introduce you to everyone.'

Lucia spun back towards the visitor.

'Matthieu isn't rostered on until Thursday,' Leonie added. 'It will give him time to sit in on radio or phone consultations and get his bearings. I want you to show him around and look after him.'

Lucia suspected the thrill of excitement that shot through her had little to do with the responsibility she was being given. She put the stack of remaining files on top of one of the cabinets, pushing them into a neat pile to hide her eager excitement. Filing could wait!

'Have you found somewhere to live?'

Leonie's question made her turn towards the new doctor. He had such a clean, fresh, handsome look about him. Maybe it was the haircut. Or the pale, clear skin, lightly tanned but not burnt to mahogany like most of the men in the tropics.

'—small flat in Lancaster Street.'

But that was where she lived! Lucia tried to penetrate the dithery fog that seemed to have invaded her mind.

'Splendid!' Leonie was saying. 'You can walk to work from there, and if you're ever in doubt about anything you can call in and see Lucia. She lives with her aunt in the big house on the corner and, although she's only been with us a few months, she knows how we like things done.'

Lucia grinned. How *you* like things done, she thought affectionately.

'Show Matthieu around now and let me get on with some work,' Leonie ordered with mock severity, and Lucia knew that her boss had guessed what she'd been thinking.

She led the man out of the office.

'Is Matthieu a French name when it's spelt that way?' she asked, then wished she could have thought of a more scintillating conversational gambit.

'It is, but the English quarter of me insists on being called Matt by friends and workmates.'

He smiled at her, a warm, conspiratorial smile that made the skin along her spine prickle with an awareness she had never felt before.

'And which quarter of you is English?' she asked, then blushed when she realised that the question was badly phrased.

Before he had time to reply the alarm that meant 'emergency flight' sounded and Susan pushed past them, heading for the operation room where the alert would be explained.

'This way! You might as well see how things happen,' Lucia said, dragging the new doctor by the arm towards the nerve centre of the building.

'You got here, then,' Jack Gregory acknowledged Matt when they met him at the door. 'I managed to get a locum for two weeks and he's out on the clinic flight today. I think Leonie's got you rostered to start later in the week so listen up. It might be you going off next time those bells ring.'

Jack moved on while Lucia and Matt paused by the door, listening to a tall woman with long straight hair explain the situation.

'It's a light plane down. Wreckage spotted by the

mail plane. Joe's got on to ''Wetherby'', the nearest property, and asked them to send out a land vehicle to check. It's hilly country and he can't land nearby so he'll stay up over the crash site to give them a guide to the location.'

Katie Watson was the radio officer, a title more by courtesy than fact now that satellite-linked telephones had superseded most of the radios in their area. As always, Lucia was impressed by her calm, matter-of-fact air. Katie always said that there was no point in panicking, but panic still stuttered to life in Lucia's heart every time the alarm sounded.

'So, what do you do?' Matt whispered, his eyes on the movement taking place around the big table at one end of the room.

'Wait!' Lucia told him, and wondered if he felt the same burning impatience to see the team swing into action that she experienced every time there were doubtful scenarios like this. 'Joe is the pilot of the mail plane. He'll contact Katie again once he's spoken to the people at ''Wetherby''. There's no point in our sending a plane out there until we know more.'

Susan had moved to stand beside them and it was she who finished the explanation.

'We can't help dead bodies,' she pointed out with what seemed to Lucia to be unnecessary brutality. 'There's no point in our dashing off into what sounds like difficult terrain if there's nothing we can do. It takes a plane away from base when it might be needed urgently somewhere else.'

Matt nodded as if he understood, and Lucia found herself hoping that he wouldn't think them callous.

'The doctor on duty at the base—that's Jack, today—

has to prioritise the call. Priority One means go now. Two means urgent but negotiate on time. Priority Three is make a time that's suitable. Sometimes a Priority Three can wait until a flight is going that way for something else,' Lucia explained as Susan moved away from them, crossing to the wall to see on the big map where the accident had taken place.

'So this would be a One or Two?' Matt asked, and Lucia could hear excitement in his voice.

'I don't think Jack will give it a classification until he knows more, but he'll alert the pilot on duty. If the pilot's not at the airport already, they'll page him. He will always be there within half an hour and will have the plane ready to go.'

She answered automatically, her mind wondering why men and women were so different. She felt fear and apprehension and a terrible anxiety for the people who might be lying out there in the middle of nowhere in excruciating pain, and this man standing beside her felt excitement!

She shifted uneasily and brushed against her charge, feeling the hardness of the muscles in his arm and the taut expectancy in his body.

Matt sensed her fear and something urged him to put his arm around her shoulders and comfort her. Hardly proper behaviour for a new staff member!

It was a fleeting thought, quickly banished when he sensed a heightened urgency in the room. Adrenalin was surging through his body—and he was only an onlooker! When he'd heard about the Royal Flying Doctor Service it had appealed to him enormously. Exciting and romantic! Dashing through the air on rescue missions! But now the challenge of it all was

becoming real and the sheer logistics of getting to
injured or sick patients hundreds of kilometres away, in
the hope of saving their lives, almost overwhelmed him.

He looked at the people gathered in the room. The
woman who had outlined the problem so concisely had
turned back to the radio. Jack Gregory was leaning over
her shoulder. The nurse who'd come in earlier, neat in
a blue skirt and floral blouse, had left the room for a
while and was now back, checking equipment in a small
carry-bag. Organised, efficient, calm! Were these people
not feeling the same rush of excitement he was? Had it
all become routine to them?

'I'm Peter Flint. You the new doctor?'

A tall, well-built man with the looks of a golden god
stopped beside him and thrust out his hand.

'I'm not here,' he added, as Matt introduced himself
and shook his hand.

'He means he's officially off duty but has popped in
to see what's on offer for morning tea,' Lucia explained,
and Matt sensed disapproval in the casual words.

'You'd miss me, beautiful, if I didn't pop in,' Peter
teased, tugging at one of the inky black curls that
cascaded around Lucia's shoulders. As the young girl
moved away from his touch Matt saw the colour flood
her clear skin and sparks of anger flicker in huge
brown eyes.

The animation and colour in her face turned her from
a very pretty girl into a beauty, but he failed to register
that in his conscious mind. For a moment he forgot the
build-up of tension behind him as a totally out-of-
character urge to hit Peter Flint swept over his body.

'I think I'll get a little closer to the action,' he said

tightly, and moved away before his body could rebel against his common sense.

'Why don't you go home and rest?' Lucia snapped at Peter, upset that Matt had moved away.

'No one to warm my bed,' Peter replied, then he, too, crossed to the table where a computer was now showing the exact location of the crash site. He paused there for a moment, spoke to Jack, then turned away and walked out of the room.

Lucia watched him go, noticing a tired slump to his broad shoulders and an unusual weariness in the way he walked. She remembered Susan's words. Did he laugh and joke and tease and flirt to hide some unhappiness? she wondered, then Jack's voice said, 'We'll go!' and the room came alive with movement.

'You want to come with us?'

Lucia heard Jack's question and saw Matt's face light up. Another adventure! That's how it would seem to him, she realised, though why that should make her feel sad she didn't know. Susan passed him the bag and ushered him out of the room through the door that led to the parking area behind the building. He turned as he walked away, and she saw him nod and smile.

She lifted her hand in a gesture of farewell and, with a deflated emptiness dogging her footsteps, returned to her filing.

'The new doctor has gone with them,' she told Leonie, who nodded and continued working through the pile of papers stacked symmetrically in front of her. The monitor on her desk would keep her informed of the progress of the flight and Katie, in touch with the crew for the entire operation, would advise 'Wetherby' of their ETA and handle any problems that might arise.

Putting Matt Laurant firmly out of her mind, Lucia returned to the mundane task of keeping records in order.

The airport was a five-minute drive from the base, and Matt looked about him with interest. He might be driving next time.

'The manager and a jackaroo from ''Wetherby'' have driven out to the crash site,' Jack explained over his shoulder as he turned into the airport gates. 'Both pilot and passenger are alive but unconscious, and trapped. No smell of fuel so Bill Wilson, the manager, has sent the young fellow back to pick us up from 'Wetherby' airstrip and Bill's stayed there—trying to free them.'

'Surely, in this day and age, no one runs out of fuel,' Susan complained.

'Faulty fuel gauge or slow leak—who knows?' Jack suggested, and Matt was impressed by his tolerance. It was important for doctors to be non-judgemental but he sometimes found it hard, especially when he knew that patients had endangered not only their own lives but the lives of others as well.

The car drew in beside a shining new hangar. Jack and Susan were out of the car before him, hurrying across the tarmac towards the small aircraft with RFDS printed proudly across its tail.

'Royal Flying Doctor Service,' he whispered to himself, giving the initials their full name. The spoken words evoked the magic and romance that had flooded his being when he'd first heard them. 'And I'm part of it!' he reminded himself, barely able to contain his excitement.

Grasping the bag he'd been given earlier, he

scrambled out and the heat burning up from the bitumen surface hit him like a tangible force. He could hear the engine revving on the plane and hurried towards it. Jack reached down and took the gear, Susan gave him a hand up and almost before the door was closed they were taxi-ing slowly away from the buildings.

'All in?'

Matt looked up from the intricacies of his seat belt and blinked. The pilot was a petite brunette and, from what he could see beneath earphones and behind a small mouthpiece, a remarkably pretty brunette at that.

'Nothing against women drivers, I hope?' Susan said with a smile.

'Nothing at all,' he assured her, looking around at the interior of the plane. If the sight of a woman pilot had surprised him, the intricate array of equipment in the plane was even more startling. It was set up like a mini emergency room at a hospital. Two stretchers down one side had oxygen tubes and monitoring equipment hung above them, while a small, portable vital-signs monitor was tucked between them. Once the patient was in the plane he could be hooked up to very sophisticated machinery.

'I believe if we can get to an accident patient within an hour, we have an excellent chance of saving him or her,' Jack—seated next to the pilot—turned back to explain, obviously aware of Matt's wonder. 'And as soon as we're up, you can swap seats with me and see the country unfold beneath you.'

The engines whined, and the plane lifted as easily as a bird.

Matt peered out of the window, then shook his head in amazement as the town disappeared and the wide sweep of blue bay with its white crescent of sand grew smaller and smaller. Then Jack was beside him, his tall figure bent forward as if moving about in the confined space was as natural to him as breathing.

'Off you go,' he said, and Matt, after a startled glance at Susan who was reading a magazine as calmly as if she was on a commuter train on her way to work in a city office, made his way forward.

'I'm Matt,' he said, sliding into the spare seat beside the pilot.

She smiled at him and removed her headset.

'Sorry!' she said. 'Shall we start again? I was tuned into the control tower at the Bay and listening for calls from either the base or ''Wetherby'' or Joe, but now I can hear you.'

He grinned at her and introduced himself again, although the sight of rolling canefields beneath them and swelling green mountains ahead had left him almost speechless.

'Admire the green,' the pilot, who had introduced herself as Allysha, told him. 'As soon as we cross to the other side of the range the country changes colour. The range acts as a watershed. Rain-clouds hit the mountains and drop all their moisture—too much some-times—so on one side it's all lush and green, while on the other it's like the bare earth of the centre.'

'Don't they get any rain out here?' he asked, as the country changed in proof of her prediction.

'Some from cyclones sweeping in over the gulf, and the occasional low that blows over the mountains. Makes good cattle country,' she explained, and Matt peered down through the Perspex towards the distant earth.

' ''Wetherby'' airstrip ahead and to the right,' Allysha told him a little later, and his eyes, accustomed now to the glare off the red earth, picked out the tiny space cleared of the low scrubby trees that dotted the landscape like a green rash.

'You can't land there,' he gasped, as they descended and circled above what seemed an impossibly small, dirt runway.

'Watch me!' she teased, lining up and dropping lower and lower. 'We give the property owners the specifications for the length and width of the strips, and it's their responsibility to keep them cleared for us.' The wheels kissed the ground, the plane jolted, rose and then steadied back onto the dirt strip. 'We actually need less length for these sophisticated machines than they did in the old days.'

Her soft voice was blurred then lost as the roar of deceleration blotted out the words.

Allysha lifted a hand-held microphone and spoke to someone—presumably reporting that they had landed safely. Peering around him, Matt could see nothing but red earth, clumpy, dry-looking grass and, on both sides of the cleared strip, the encroaching trees. It was from them that the cloud of red dust appeared, rolling towards them as Allysha turned the plane to face back the way they had landed and braked to a halt.

Slowly a vehicle emerged like a mirage from the centre of the cloud. A rough-looking four-wheel-drive, red with the dust that seemed to be everywhere.

'That was the easy part,' Jack told him as he hurried from the plane, out into the searing heat. 'Now we go cross-country with young Andy here, who drives the way Allysha flies—straight over the top of everything.'

'Load these into the car,' Susan said, handing him the solid case again. 'We take drugs and these bags with splints, plasma, fluids, dressings and shock trousers with us. When you come back I'll pass you the lightweight stretchers, neck collars and spine boards. They are in a different pack.'

Matt hurried to the dusty vehicle with his first load, passed it to Jack, who was discussing the accident with the young driver, then jogged back towards the plane.

'Tell Susan to bring the monitor,' Jack called after him.

The monitor? he wondered. Was it battery operated? Portable enough to be carried with them?

He saw Susan leave the plane, already carrying the small monitor he'd noticed earlier.

'I left the stretchers on the ground,' she told him as he hurried past her. 'And don't run around too much in this heat—you'll dehydrate and collapse on us.'

'Do you come with us?' he asked Allysha, who had left her seat and was sitting in the doorway, her feet dangling out of the plane.

'Not this time,' she said. 'It's an area of bad reception and out of mobile phone range. Bill's car has CB radio and I'll stay here by our receiver in case Jack needs to relay information back to base or be patched through to a specialist at the hospital.'

He nodded, understanding that it was a true team effort and an important part of that effort was keeping the lines of communication open.

Picking up the bulky packs which Susan had left on the ground, he walked carefully back to the others.

As he reached them Jack slapped a battered old hat on his head.

'No one walks around out here without one,' he warned. 'Get used to it.'

They swung into the cabin of the vehicle and set off, travelling through the trees in an apparently aimless way. Matt clung to the hand-grip to steady himself as they jolted over boulders, logs and ant-beds, down into gullies and, metal screaming in protest, up out of them again.

Somewhere ahead of them were two injured people. Would the three of them be able to save these strangers? They bounced over a pothole big enough to hide a bullock, and beside him even the imperturbable Susan gave a little gasp of horror.

Again he felt the blood rush that signaled the alertness that only great challenges could provide. This was the ultimate adventure, he thought, high on excitement, and then, as they lurched sickeningly sideways, he wondered how often a rescue team needed rescuing.

CHAPTER TWO

'IT'S just through these trees,' Andy told them after what seemed like hours but was only ten minutes of painful discomfort.

Matt peered ahead and then, with a sickening jolt in the pit of his stomach, he spotted the wreck. It looked like a disabled insect, thrown carelessly down onto the ground by a ravaging bird.

'It must have landed wheels first, which is a miracle in this country,' Jack pointed out. 'That's why the cabin is more or less intact.'

'Then hit those trees. That's where the wing sheered off and brought the body around and into that gully,' Andy explained, one hand pointing to the trees while his other steered them casually over more scrub towards the disabled plane. 'Bill and I rigged up a bit of shade over it,' he added as they skidded to a halt, sending red dust billowing into the air behind them.

'Great for open wounds, this dust,' Susan muttered to Matt. 'We take that bag with oxygen, monitoring equipment, drips and drugs with us.' She waved her hand towards the bulky bag Jack was carrying. 'And this one with dressings, inflatable splints and anti-shock trousers. Leave everything else in this torture chamber of a vehicle while we have a look.'

Matt relieved her of the second bag and followed, suddenly uncertain about a lot of things.

'I've freed the passenger's legs but left him sitting

in the seat, thinking he'd be more comfortable that way. Brought morphine and bandages out of our kit, but he's been out like a light so I didn't give him anything. Reckon he hit his head on the window either when they landed or when they hit the tree. His right leg's busted and his ankle doesn't look too good, but there's not a lot of blood. The other chap was moaning something awful, so I gave him a shot.'

Matt frowned. Gave him a shot? Of morphine? There was no time to ask, but how did this farmer have access to morphine? The man Susan had introduced as Bill Wilson explained these details in a laconic monotone, as if a disaster like this were an everyday occurrence. Jack was examining the pilot, who was wedged into a seemingly impossible space.

'There's bleeding somewhere but it can't be arterial or he'd be dead by now,' he said as he straightened up. 'Will stretchers fit in the back of your Land Rover, Bill?'

Matt looked at the filthy vehicle. Surely not!

'So long as someone sits in there and holds onto them tight,' the lean, tanned man replied. 'I'll dump some of the gear and push the back seats down.'

He turned away to re-organise his vehicle into a makeshift ambulance.

'Send Andy over with the two stretchers, then drive up closer to the plane,' Jack called after him. 'If we can secure a chain through here—' he indicated part of the front cowling '—we might be able to use your winch to peel the metal back, hook on to the engine and shift it enough to free this chap's legs.'

Susan had moved around to the other side of the plane and was examining the passenger. Matt stood uncertainly, wishing he could be given a job yet pleased, at the moment, to be an onlooker. It gave him time to absorb what was happening—to get the feel of the methodical way these two professionals went about their jobs.

'The important thing is to take time to assess the situation,' Jack said, almost echoing his thoughts. 'Then give yourself tasks—one step at a time.'

He was bent over the pilot now, the bag he'd carried open at his feet. After a few minutes he waved Matt closer.

'His pulse is high, blood pressure low. I'll put him on oxygen and start an IV for fluid replacement.' Jack worked as he spoke, with an efficient certainty. 'Now, we hook him up to the monitor and I'll get you to keep an eye on him while Andy and I try to free his legs.'

Matt peered in at the unconscious man, and horror clamped its hands around his stomach. There was blood around but, as Jack had said, not much. Yet the instrument panel of the plane was sitting in the man's lap, wedging him tightly into the seat.

'My main concern is that the weight of the engine might be acting as pressure on damaged blood vessels,' Jack explained. 'Get gloves on, grab a pad from the bag and be ready in case there's an artery torn or severed.'

Glad to be busy, Matt followed these instructions then divided his attention between observations of the patient and watching the intricate business of freeing him.

The thick chain bit into the light cladding of the plane and the winch on the vehicle peeled it back effortlessly.

'Can't have happened too long before Joe spotted them,' Bill muttered, waving a hand he had burnt slightly while attaching a cable to the engine. 'Engine's still flamin' hot.'

Matt turned back to his patient and tried to ease one hand between the engine block and the man's legs to prevent further damage as it lifted clear. He heard the whining of the winch, then a tearing and grinding as the once beautiful little plane was torn apart.

The warmth of blood on his hand alerted him. Jack had guessed correctly. Before the engine had dropped onto the top of the pilot's thighs, something had sliced through skin and muscle as cleanly as a surgeon's knife and bright arterial blood was spurting upward.

Matt reacted automatically, jamming the pad into place and feeling into the man's groin with his free hand to try to find the femoral artery and halt the flow.

'Good man! I'll wrap the wound and check his legs.' There was silence for a few moments before Jack continued, 'You can relax that pressure. There doesn't appear to be a fracture in the femur but there's crepitus in the knee. How's he holding?'

Matt glanced at the monitor. 'Systolic pressure has dropped to eighty.'

'Too low! We've got to get him back as quickly as we can. Unfold one of the stretchers—you'll see how they work, it's all Velcro tabs—then slot the metal frame together when it's laid out flat. Put it as close as you can to the plane so the monitor leads will reach it. I'm going to splint his leg in a bent position, stabilise his neck and spine and then we'll lift him across and fasten him in.'

Matt bent over the pack Andy had dropped behind the plane and found it undid as easily as Jack had said it would.

'There are more Velcro straps in the hold-all. Once we've got him on the stretcher we need to immobilise his head,' Jack told him, and he turned and dug inside the bag he had carried across to the plane.

From behind the wreckage he could hear Susan giving instructions to Bill. This is like ambulance or paramedic work, he realised. And to think I've never given those men enough credit for what they do!

With the stretcher spread like a black shadow on the red earth, he straightened up and noticed that Jack had secured a neck brace around the unconscious man's neck and slipped a spinal corset from beneath the brace down to his hips, securing it in place with Velcro tapes.

'That should help,' Jack said quietly. 'Now, I'll stop the drip until we get him into the vehicle but keep the oxygen going. Using these small bottles, you can usually tuck them into the patient's clothing while you transfer him or her and then secure them onto the stretcher. With the drip, I don't like to risk tubing coming adrift or causing needle-stick injuries as we move him.'

Matt nodded, hoping that he would remember all the practical advice Jack was offering.

'Now, we swivel him around and lift him carefully. He's got left tib and fib fractures. I haven't been able to assess the damage to his ankles but we'll do a secondary assessment and can splint the left leg once we've got him back on the plane. How's your man, Susan?'

It was the first communication between them, although Susan had earlier given a running commentary of what she had found and how she was treating her patient.

'I'm strapping him in ready to go, Jack, but I don't like the concussion. There's a swelling above the left temple—where he probably banged against the window—reaction to painful stimuli, unequal pupils, with one fixed and one dilated, but no fluid from the nose or ears.'

Jack sighed.

'Possible third cranial nerve involvement or eye trauma? Let's get them both home,' he said quietly. 'I don't fancy doing emergency brain surgery on the plane.'

Matt felt shock jolt through him, then realised that the man was joking—making light of a situation that had possibly turned out far better than any of them could have hoped. He was still considering the atrocious injuries they might have found when Jack spoke again.

'Andy, see if you can open the luggage locker or get your hand behind the seats. They may have been carrying overnight bags with personal things in them that will help in identification and be useful in hospital. Then carry the infusion bag for Susan—she'll show you how.'

With everyone helping, the two stretchers were loaded into the back of the vehicle. An old tarpaulin and some bags had been spread on the metal floor but Matt thought of the bouncing, jostling drive they'd had from the RFDS plane to the wreckage and shuddered.

'Sit in here and hold the head of the stretcher as tight as you can,' Bill told him, pushing him into the back through one of the rear doors. 'Grab those bags from Andy.' Matt reached out and took the overnight bags Andy had rescued from the plane and a small leather folder that seemed to hold maps and lists of regulations. He packed them under his body, then reached out again to take the infusion bag that Andy was still holding as high as possible above the patient.

'Jack, you sit in the back and keep a hand on the second stretcher and, Andy, you walk behind,' Bill con-

tinued. 'I won't be going too fast, so see if you can
steady both of them.'

Listening to the quiet voice giving such concise
orders, Matt understood that this was real teamwork,
with the one who knew most about each part of the
operation taking charge when appropriate. The excitement he'd felt earlier surged again and as the second
stretcher was loaded he reached for the monitor propped
beside the unconscious man and turned it so that he and
Jack could both keep an eye on the small screen.

Andy seemed to accept his position as walker without
fuss and obediently dropped in behind, one hand on
each of the stretchers. Jack stacked the bags on the front
seat, hoisted Susan in on top of them and then came
around to clamber in and squat at the head of the second
stretcher.

'All in, Bill,' he said, and the strange conveyance
started slowly on its way, easing over the logs they had
taken with such bravado earlier and crawling in and out
of the gullies which Andy had dashed across.

The trip back seemed endless, with no familiar land-
marks to show that they had been this way before, but,
as they came out of the trackless scrub, Matt realised
that Bill had known exactly where he was going. The
shining plane stood only metres from where they
emerged and Allysha had the engine running.

The transfer was sure and swift, the stretchers
snapped into their fixed position in the plane with an
efficiency that came from long years of practice.
Infusion bags were hooked onto clips that dangled from
a track in the ceiling of the plane, and oxygen was
readjusted.

'Ready?' Allysha asked, and Jack gave the all-clear,

strapping himself into the seat beside his patient before reaching out to feel the pressure in the inflated splint on Susan's patient.

'Always remember air-splints and anti-shock garments need pressure released before take-off,' he said casually to Matt. 'Even in pressurised aircraft like the King Air, pressure is increased by altitude. I inflate splints to get to the plane and deflate them slightly before we take off, but MAST gear we keep at a lower pressure until we're in the air. If the patient's blood pressure drops we can inflate them further once we're heading for home.'

Allysha taxied along the dirt strip and lifted the plane gently into the air. Now that they were airborne the activity accelerated.

'Next we do a full assessment,' Jack explained. 'I'll splint this chap's lower leg first but Susan will be getting started if you want to watch her.'

Matt eased his way out of his seat and manoeuvred past Jack. Susan was checking the patient's head for signs of bruising or contusions, her fingers running gently but firmly over the facial bones.

'This is a look-and-feel examination and it's a whole lot easier with a conscious patient who can at least tell you where things hurt.' She continued down the body, visualising and palpating, testing reflexes and reactions and noting down her findings.

'You do all this as easily as if you were in a casualty room in a real hospital,' he muttered, wondering if he would ever display such sureness.

'We've both been at it for a long time. Jack's been here seven years,' Susan explained, 'and I started when this base opened. My husband, Eddie, is the chief pilot here.' She blushed, then smiled. 'We're a Flying Doctor true romance.'

Matt grinned at the admission then, seeing Jack settle back into his seat and start filling in a sheet similar to the one Susan had been using, he moved back up towards the doctor. Squatting between Jack and the patient, he looked at the unconscious man.

'Should we remove his boots and check his ankles?'

'I've been wondering that myself. They'll have to be cut off at some stage but, at the moment, if there's a crush injury involving either ankle or foot the boots might be holding things together. I think we might leave it until he's in hospital with an orthopedic specialist standing by. I'm getting onto the hospital now, so listen and remind me if I leave anything out.'

To Matt's amazement, he lifted the receiver off a phone attached to the front cabin wall and pressed a memory button as casually as any doctor in a suburban surgery.

'They don't work in all the areas we cover and we were out of range on 'Wetherby' but once we're up here it's no trouble,' he explained while the switchboard at Rainbow Bay hospital connected him to Casualty.

Matt listened while Jack gave a clear and concise description of the two men's injuries, and explained which specialists he thought should be on stand-by to receive the patients.

'Does an ambulance meet the plane?' he asked as Jack finished.

'Yes. We work in with them all the time. The pilot radios our ETA to base and the radio officer on duty alerts the ambulance. With the mobile phone network growing wider and wider we are using radio less and less, but certain procedures have been in place for so long it's difficult to know just how to change them so that we still work as efficiently.'

Matt frowned, unable to understand what Jack was saying. The older man checked his patient again and then, as if talking to himself, continued.

'The doctor has the mobile phone, but he's often busy during the flight. I mean, he's not going to stop halfway through a premi delivery on board an aircraft to phone home for an ambulance. At the moment our system works without a hitch and I'm tempted to say that if it isn't broken, why fix it?'

He made another notation on the sheet, then opened the leather wallet and the overnight bags, searching for something that might identify their two patients. Matt felt a change in the engine vibrations and slid back into his seat in time to see the sparkling waters of the bay spread out in welcome.

Once the transfers to the ambulance were completed and the vehicle sped away, Matt felt a strange emptiness.

'It's a bit like being on the emergency ward where your patients get whipped away to other wards and no longer belong to you,' Jack said, again picking up on his thoughts with uncanny accuracy.

'But you do it all the time,' Matt said. 'Is there no continuity of patients?'

Susan emerged from the plane with a bundle of dirty linen in time to hear the question.

'No continuity of patients?' she scoffed. 'This emergency stuff might add a little variety to life but your regular routine is as boring or as interesting as any other GP's. You just go to a different office each day and you get there by light aircraft, not car.'

Matt blinked. He knew about the regular clinics but he hadn't thought of them as ordinary GP work.

'You'll have plenty of regular patients,' Jack assured him. 'And there's nothing to stop you going up to the hospital to check on patients we've evacuated if you want to follow up on them. Now, come on, team, let's get back to base and eat before someone decides they need us somewhere else.'

As they drove back through the wide streets Matt tried to recall all that had happened and to memorise the sequence of events.

'It's still the basic A B C with accident cases, isn't it?' he said to Jack. 'Airways, breathing, circulation— then get on with the rest of the jobs in order of importance.'

Jack nodded.

'And the most important thing with accident victims is to look at the wreckage. Try to see what's happened so you can imagine what forces were applied to the victim's body.

'With a head-on collision there's likely to be comminuted fractures of the lower limbs, for instance, and possibly crush injuries to the chest from the steering-wheel. In those cases you must always be prepared to do a needle decompression or a chest intubation. In a car that's rolled over suspect internal injuries, spleen, kidney or liver damage. The seat belt could have saved the bloke's life by keeping him from being thrown out but it could have caused problems as well.'

'And always assume neck injuries in any car accident,' Susan added, and Matt nodded, happily absorbing all that these professionals could offer from their years of experience.

They pulled into the space behind the base, and Matt looked at his watch. Two-thirty! They'd been gone for nearly five hours, yet it seemed like only moments ago that they had driven out of the car park. Did Lucia work full time? he wondered, then smiled to himself. For a fellow who was determined to stay footloose and fancy free for the next few years it was a strange thought to be entertaining.

'That was the easy part,' Jack said as they walked back inside. 'Now the paperwork begins. It's enough to drive most men to drink. All our operational reports are done in duplicate: one copy goes to the hospital and the other stays with us. Using our copy, we work out what we've used from base supplies and the plane supplies, then requisition replacements.'

'So the next person called out doesn't get to an emergency and find there's no long air-splint?' Matt found himself fascinated by the organisational details of the operation but, when he glimpsed Lucia walking across the far end of the corridor, his attention wavered.

'Exactly! Now come and eat,' Jack suggested, leading the way into a small kitchen that obviously did duty as a staff-room as well. Wooden chairs were grouped around a square pine table and a clutter of magazines, ranging from *Current Therapeutics* to Superman comics, were flung haphazardly across it.

'How are your patients?'

Matt spun around and once again something in Lucia's voice, a vulnerability he found hard to understand, made him want to reach out and touch her—to reassure her in some way.

'Both at the hospital by now, with specialists hovering

over them,' Jack told her gently, as if he, too, felt protective towards the young woman.

Lucia smiled her relief, then shifted a little uncomfortably when she realised that Matt was watching her with a puzzled expression in his eyes.

'I've put the next fortnight's rosters on your desk,' she said hurriedly to Jack, trying to ignore the fluttery feeling Matt's presence was causing. 'Will—' She hesitated. 'Matt' sounded too...friendly, somehow, for someone she'd just met and 'Dr Laurant' sounded too formal. 'Does the new doctor have a desk?' she continued desperately. 'I've a set of rosters for him—' She turned and smiled apologetically at Matt. 'For you!' she added.

Jack smiled at her and she relaxed—slightly.

'Put his roster on the locum's desk. The locum's on an overnight clinic run, then off duty for a day and on call for his final day so Matt might as well take over his desk now.'

He walked across to the refrigerator and pulled out two packs of sandwiches, tossing them onto the table.

'Have some sandwiches. It's all help-yourself here,' he explained to Matt. 'The water in the urn is always hot, cups in that top cupboard, coffee, tea and sugar on the bench and there's usually food in the fridge. We never know when we're going to need a feed.'

Lucia watched the new doctor prowl around the room as if familiarising himself with this unfamiliar environment. He selected a mug and was measuring coffee into it when Jack spoke again, this time to her.

'Perhaps if Leonie doesn't need you for the rest of the afternoon you could show Matt his desk and finish his tour of the base.'

He paused and smiled before he added, 'And don't forget to point out the cupboard where all the files and order forms are kept. He might as well learn the realities of the job right from the start!'

'I don't mind paperwork,' Matt protested, and Lucia found herself repeating the mundane words over in her head, trying to capture what it was that fascinated her about his voice. 'Although I thought maybe computers would be taking over a lot of that by now.'

'They are,' Jack groaned. 'But the little blighters won't absorb the information out of the air. Some poor, overworked human still has to feed it all to them. Fortunately Lucia here, for all her sweet, helpless looks, is a computer whizz and she's usually willing to give people who grew up without them a hand to fathom their mysteries.'

Surprised by the unexpected praise, Lucia shrugged.

'I spent a lot of time playing computer games so I'm not afraid of them,' she explained, concerned that Matt might think her an electronic genius. 'I'll go and tell Mrs Cooper what I'm doing and come back when you've had your lunch.'

Embarrassed by Jack's words and confused by her reaction to the new staff member, she hurried away.

Surely she couldn't be attracted to the man?

She shook her head, trying to banish the thought. He was here on a temporary basis and then, like all the other overseas staff who came to work for the Flying Doctor Service, he would be winging his way back home again. She knew herself well enough to know that her happiness lay in her home and family—or very close to that home! Especially since the accident that had left her mother so incapacitated.

She blinked away the stupid tears that thinking of the accident still produced, and walked calmly into Leonie's office to explain what Jack had asked her to do.

'Sounds fine to me, but don't try to tell him too much at once. We don't want him suffering from information overload before he's officially on board.'

Leonie smiled at her and Lucia felt a rush of gratitude towards this woman who had offered her so much.

'I'll try to keep it simple,' she promised and turned away, walking back towards the lunch-room very calmly although her feet ached with a desire to skip along the corridor.

'That's about it,' she said two hours later, locking the doors on the big cupboard in the back-up equipment room. 'Most of the equipment is kept at the airport because staff on call for emergency flights go straight there after hours and on weekends. Coming to the base first would be a waste of time.'

Matt followed her through to the radio room, where she returned the keys to the keyboard hanging on the wall near the door.

'"About it"!' he protested. 'If I remember one quarter of what you've told me I'll be doing well!'

'It will all become routine in a few weeks,' she promised, then smiled shyly when she realised that he was looking at her intently.

'You've got the most sensational eyelashes,' he muttered, shaking his head as if the words had come out against his will.

The personal remark shocked her into momentary immobility. She caught her breath then said lightly, 'You should see my oldest brother's. They are twice as long as mine! His wife says it's most unfair that a man should have got them.'

She was babbling on, trying to defuse whatever it was in the air between them. She tried to calm the agitation she felt but Matt Laurant's presence was doing the strangest things to her equilibrium.

'Well, it's time to head for home,' she continued, feeling more breathless by the moment. She led the way back to the front office, picked up her shoulder-bag and collected her hat from the pegs by the door.

'Do I have to sign out or say goodbye to anyone?' he asked, and she shook her head.

'Jack and Susan left about an hour ago. They're still on duty but will be on call. If they're needed the after-hours answering service will put through medical calls to Jack or page them if they are needed for an evacuation flight. Mrs Cooper usually leaves about four o'clock. She has two children to supervise after school, so she starts and finishes early.'

Matt nodded, then smiled at her.

'So it's you and I, and—if I remember rightly—you live in my street. We can walk home together.'

He sounded so delighted by the prospect that she felt a warm pleasure sweep across her body and knew she had found a friend. As they walked out into the warm tropical dusk, Rainbow Bay took on a luminescence she had never noticed before. The red ball of the sun was poised above the mountains to the west, blazing its final defiance before it disappeared, to be reborn at dawn from the glowing waters of the bay.

'I wonder if you could explain to me how to get to the hospital.' Matt's voice broke into her thoughts, and she turned to him in surprise.

'Are you all right?' Even as her words came out she knew that they were ridiculous, but he chuckled reassuringly and explained.

'I know it's stupid and I'm certain I won't feel the same way about every patient I attend, but I would like to see those two men—or at least assure myself that they are doing as well as could be expected.'

Lucia was pleased but not surprised. She had learnt that most of the doctors felt the same way, and getting follow-up information on patients was often part of her job.

'If you can wait until after dinner you could walk up there with me,' she suggested, leading the way out of the base grounds and across the road to Lancaster Street. She hoped that the silly excitement she felt wasn't obvious to this man, who was still a stranger.

'You're going to the hospital?' He fell in beside her as he spoke, sounding amazed by the coincidence. 'Is a friend sick? Or a member of your family?'

'No, no one close to me,' she assured him with a chuckle. 'But I walk up there most evenings.'

She hesitated, wanting to explain but anxious lest she bore him with such trivial details of her life. They were walking slowly and she felt so at ease with him that she didn't want to spoil it.

'I visit our clinic patients,' she said, and decided to leave it at that. But she reckoned without Matt's curiosity.

'Visit clinic patients?' he echoed, coming to a halt beneath a scented ti tree.

Lucia stopped with him, and turned to look into his face.

'It started soon after I began doing work experience

at the base,' she told him. 'Jimmy Carew, a six-year-old whose parents live on a cattle property over near the gulf, was brought in with appendicitis. It had already burst—'

'Peritonitis?' Matt asked, and Lucia nodded.

'It meant he was in hospital a lot longer than antici- pated. His mother, who had been frantic about sending him off in the plane by himself in the first place, became so upset she was making herself ill.'

'Couldn't she have come to town with him? Doesn't the plane usually bring a relation?'

Lucia heard the doubt in his voice and, beneath that, the caring.

'Yes, a relation can sometimes come, particularly if it's a child, but in Jimmy's case his mother couldn't leave the property. There's been a drought—'

'I saw that!' he said quietly.

'And with no feed on the property James Carew had taken his breeding stock on the road, trying to keep them alive on the dry grass along the verges. Mary stayed at home to keep the place going. She had one man working with her and three other kids to mind. There was no way she could leave or James get home to take over while she visited Jimmy.'

'So you took on the job?' he asked, his blue eyes warm with what looked like admiration.

Lucia squirmed. 'It wasn't much effort,' she pro- tested. 'I was new in town and had nothing else to do, and after I'd visited him the first time I liked Jimmy so much I'd have gone back even if his mother hadn't been so far away.'

She turned away from the warmth in his eyes, walking slowly on towards her aunt's house.

'And is Jimmy still in hospital?' he asked as he drew alongside her again. She glanced at him and saw the teasing smile lurking in the corners of his mobile, neat-lipped mouth.

'Of course not,' she said, 'but I found I enjoyed the visit and, when you consider that all the patients we bring in for medical treatment are a long way from their homes and families, it seemed a worthwhile thing to do.'

'You must be a very caring person, Lucia,' he said. 'Perhaps you should have been a nurse or a doctor.'

The words spilt into her soul, destroying the peace and harmony of their stroll homeward and jolting too many memories back into Lucia's mind.

'No, no, I could never have done that,' she cried, far too vehemently. 'This is where I live.' She pushed open the gate and ducked behind it, as if the flimsy wooden palings were a shield and the house beyond her a refuge. 'I usually leave at seven, so come up when you're ready,' she mumbled, and turned and fled to the safety of the wide verandas of Aunt Steph's house.

Matt watched her retreat with total bewilderment. What had he said to upset her? He replayed the conversation in his head but could find no clue. Regret that he might have unknowingly hurt her in some way teased at his mind. Suddenly he knew that he would never want to hurt Lucia. Not in any way! For any reason!

'Tread carefully, Matt,' he warned himself as he turned and walked back towards the house where he had taken a small, detached flat.

CHAPTER THREE

LUCIA was dressed and waiting on the front veranda ten minutes before Matt arrived, and she spent the time reproving herself for her behaviour. She had mentioned the new doctor casually to her aunt, but had not been able to explain that he was going to walk up to the hospital with her.

It was as if it was a secret she needed to hug to herself for a little longer. But why? For what reason? She shrugged away the silent questions. The whole situation was nonsensical! She was going to show him how to get to the hospital, that was all. Nothing more! And she certainly didn't want her curious and unpredictable aunt reading something into a casual, chance arrangement.

The gate squeaked its warning of a visitor and she hurried down the steps, anxious to intercept him and get away from the house.

'And who is it you visit at the moment?' he asked, as they fell into step together on the grassy footpath.

'Carol Benson first,' Lucia told him, breathing deeply in an attempt to contain the excitement that bubbled within her. Not that breathing deeply helped! All that did was intensify the lemony tang of his aftershave, which was acting on her nerves like an intoxicant.

'She and her husband work a small tin mine out beyond Wooli, which is a little over an hour's flying time from here.'

'They actually mine tin? And make a living?'

Matt's incredulity made Lucia smile, but his questions hadn't stopped.

'And is all distance measured by flying time?' he added, turning towards her as they walked through the yellow wash of a streetlight, as if he might read the answers in her face.

'Either flying time or driving time,' she explained, taking the last question first. 'The distance might only be a few hundred kilometres but if it's over rough terrain it could be an all-day journey and, yes,' she assured him, 'people do mine tin and make a living from it, but most of the mines seem to be in very inaccessible places.'

'Which brings us back to Mrs Benson,' he murmured. Lucia heard a hint of laughter in his voice and smiled at him. It was so good to have a friend. Their feet slowed as he half turned and smiled back. White teeth gleamed behind the pale lips and his eyes, their colour lost in the gathering darkness, seemed to glint a secret delight.

Lucia felt her chest tighten, while her heart cavorted madly within the restricted space.

'Carol is pregnant,' she said, forcing the words out through stiff lips in the hope that she might return to normal if she pretended hard enough. 'She went across to Wooli for a clinic check-up last week and the flight sister on duty found her blood pressure was right up.'

'My blood pressure would be up if I had to drive over the kind of country we drove over today,' Matt suggested, and Lucia felt the tension ease from her body.

'I suppose that doesn't help,' she agreed, 'but Carol's ankles were very swollen and the test strip showed proteinuria. . .' She hesitated, remembering that she was talking to a trained medico, then added, 'I only know what I feed into the computer, and the layman things the patients themselves tell me.'

'You sound very knowledgeable,' he assured her. 'How far into the pregnancy is she? Did they suspect hypertension? Or pre-eclampsia?'

'About twenty-four weeks,' Lucia told him, although her mind was wondering how words like 'pre-eclampsia' could sound so fascinating when ever so softly accented.

'Was this the first sign of high blood pressure?'

Typical doctor! I'm thinking of accents, and he's diagnosing a patient he hasn't even met. But she grinned to herself, enjoying his company—even if the conversation was so medically orientated.

'The specialist thought it could be mild pre-eclampsia,' she told him. 'If she'd lived on this street with a GP half a block away I'm certain she would have been treated and told to go home and rest. The doctor could have monitored her daily, not with a once-a-month clinic visit.'

'Living in town she could have had more exhaustive tests, I suppose. Normally an obstetrician would order a full blood count, serum uric acid concentration, electrolytes and creatinine, liver function tests, a full urinalysis and a twenty-four hour urinary protein assessment.'

Lucia heard the exhaustive list and smiled, realising he was muttering the words to himself as a self-test of his own knowledge—a reassurance that he still remembered the things he'd learned years ago as a student.

'And foetal monitoring is far easier in a hospital,' he added, then frowned as if there was a segment still

missing from a diagnosis of a patient he had never seen.
'There's something else,' he said, and she could see
him straining after an elusive memory. 'A rare disorder
that's usually fatal if undiagnosed. I'm certain it can
present as pre-eclampsia.'

He thought for a moment, then seemed to become
aware of his company and surroundings. They had
slowed to an amble.

'I'll have to look it up,' he said, with a rueful half-
smile that did strange things to her heartbeat.

'Did I tell you she was expecting twins?' she asked,
trying to pretend that she was as interested in the medical problem as he obviously was.

Matt gave a long, slow whistle. 'No wonder they
brought her in and admitted her to hospital. As well as
doing all the tests, they can take immediate action if
eclampsia looks like developing.'

They walked on in silence for a while, until the bright
lights of the hospital were clearly visible on a small rise
ahead of them.

'But when she's had the twins?' he asked, and Lucia
hesitated, unable to understand what he meant. She
glanced at him, seeing the neat shape of his skull outlined against the lights ahead of them and the clean look
of his profile as he turned towards her.

'Surely she cannot take newborn babies out to a place
that is over an hour's flying time from civilisation?
How will she manage them on her own? What if they
become ill?'

Lucia smiled at his concern.

'It's for people like the Bensons that the Flying
Doctor Service exists,' she explained. 'Wooli, an aboriginal settlement, is only about an hour away by car.

There's a hospital at Wooli with a nursing sister and a health worker. In a real emergency, if it was co-ordinated properly, the plane could be there by the time Carol arrived at the hospital.'

'You make it sound so simple,' he said softly, 'but an hour is a long time for a mother to be worrying about her child.'

'And how often must women wait more than an hour in the out-patients' department at a city hospital?' she teased. 'Besides, Carol has a drug chest and a radio that can connect her to the base. She can have a radio consultation with a doctor if she's worried, which is something the pioneering women couldn't do. They really were on their own until the invention of the pedal radio and the formation of the Flying Doctors.'

She smiled at his surprised expression but knew that they'd have to continue the conversation and explanations some other time.

'Come on or they'll be pushing visitors out before we get there.'

She moved away from him, away from the strange allure she felt when she looked at him, and led the way swiftly up the gentle slope of the hill and into the glaring lights and bustle of the hospital.

'And is she your only patient?' he asked while they waited at Reception to find out where the injured men had been taken.

'No, I've three on my list at the moment, but I'll spend most time with Carol. She hates being here and is chafing to get home although, deep down, she must know she's going to have to stay in town—either in hospital or boarding somewhere—until the babies arrive.'

Matt nodded. In the brightly lit foyer he could see his guide properly and realised how attractive she was looking. A strappy white dress made her smooth skin seem a light golden brown, a glowing, healthy colour that drew his fingers like a magnet. Her luxuriant dark curls hung to her shoulders but were pushed back from her forehead and temples by a wide white band, so that the darkness framed her heart-shaped face and emphasised the neatly arched brows above the profound depths of her dark, velvety eyes.

'. . .take you there.'

He realised that someone was speaking but he had been studying Lucia's lips, shiny with a colourless gloss, and he was certain they hadn't moved.

'Ward Four, Lucia,' the voice said, and he was reasonably certain that the words were a repetition.

He saw her start and wondered if she had been as lost in contemplation of him as he had been of her, but chided himself for such a stupid thought. Why should she be attracted to a total stranger? She was just a friendly girl, a fellow worker, going out of her way to make the newcomer feel at home.

'Lifts over here,' she said, threading her way through the people who criss-crossed the open space. But there'd been a hint of colour in her cheeks as she spoke and his right hand had lifted, wanting to feel that warmth and brush against the satiny skin.

He clenched his hand into a fist and followed the bobbing black curls. She had shied away from him earlier when he'd made an unwary personal comment, and instinct told him that she would retreat even further from physical contact. It was as if there was something 'untouched' about her.

'Your two patients are on the fourth floor and my first stop is on the third. When you get out of the lift, ask at the nurses' station and someone will show you the way.'

They stepped into the lift, making way for a stream of other visitors and staff. Lucia checked that the lights for floors three and four were illuminated on the control panel, then turned towards him.

'I usually stay for two hours,' she said quietly, looking up into the clear eyes that regarded her with such steady intensity. 'Will you be able to find your way home?'

She hadn't wanted to suggest that he tried, but knew that it was unfair to keep him hanging around the hospital for hours after his first day at work. He smiled, his eyes crinkling with amusement so that the blue was intensified.

'I think I can fill in two hours in a hospital,' he said. 'I worked in Perth for three months when I first arrived in Australia, saving money for my bike ride, but since then I've been out of touch. I'll just stalk along the corridors and absorb some antiseptic and ether back into my bloodstream.'

'A secret sniffer?' she suggested, smiling a little at her own joke. He was so easy to talk to—such fun!

'Maybe,' he said, returning her smile in a way that made her heart hesitate in mid-beat then hammer harder to make up the lost rhythm. 'And you've just missed your stop! Will you ride all the way up and back down, or are there stairs?'

Heat zoomed into Lucia's cheeks. How could she have been so distracted? She led the scramble of bodies out of the lift on the fourth floor, gabbled something incoherent to Matt and dashed between the closing doors of a lift going down.

What is the matter with you? her mind shrieked but, as she left the second lift and headed for the ward where Carol was spending her exile, no easy answer dropped from heaven to relieve the strange symptoms she was suffering.

It couldn't possibly be love, she told herself. She'd loved Daniel, of course, and been devastated by his death but they'd only been fifteen! Only kissed a few times in a tentative, exploratory way. And she'd known him for ever, not for one day!

She loved her parents and her brothers and sometimes—because he was kind and gentle and under-standing—she thought she loved Anthony but no one had ever sent her heart spinning, like a top, or made her feel hot and cold at the same time or so confused that she could scarcely make rational conversation.

'And what's put a sparkle into your eyes?'

The question brought her thumping back down to earth. Carol was sitting up in bed, smiling mischiev-ously at her.

'Sparkle?' she echoed, even more dismayed to dis-cover that whatever ailed her was visible to others.

'Sparkle,' Carol confirmed. 'Not to mention colour in your cheeks. And don't bother telling me it was walking up here in the summer heat. That's more likely to drain you to a shadowy whiteness.'

She shifted her legs and patted the edge of the bed, inviting Lucia to sit. 'Did you meet a handsome new doctor in the lift? Or did one of the visitors ask you for a date? You should say yes, you know. Your mother didn't send you up to town so you could spend every evening visiting people in hospital. She wanted you to get about a bit—meet other young people—hang out, and all that stuff!'

Lucia smiled. The good thing about visiting Carol was that she did ninety per cent of the talking. Whether it was because she had no one but her husband to talk to when she was at home and she was making the most of a new audience or whether she talked non-stop all the time, Lucia didn't know.

'I did "hang out", as you put it, one night,' she said, glad to have got past the 'sparkle' without further questioning. 'I went to a disco with a cousin and the fellow I was dancing with passed out on the floor in front of me, then the strobe lights gave me a migraine and four drunk teenagers followed us home shouting suggestive remarks.'

'But that might just have been a bad place to start,' Carol protested, 'or an unfortunate night to go there. You'll have to go again, or find a quieter nightclub.'

She shifted her bulk into a more comfortable position. Lucia suspected that her new friend had been over-weight before the pregnancy started, and wondered if that could have contributed to the problems she was experiencing now.

'Maybe I will,' she said to quieten Carol's concern, and then asked, 'And what did the doctor say today?'

It was her usual diversionary tactic. By rights the next half-hour of her visit should be taken up with the latest report on Carol's condition, enlivened by the woman's salty humour and scandalous opinions of the medical staff.

'. . .so on Tuesday I should be able to move into the hostel and although Bill will come down for the last six weeks in case these nuisancy kids decide to come early—which I sincerely hope they will do—I'll still have a few months of knocking about this place on my own.'

'I won't stop visiting you and, for a change, you might be able to come to my place,' Lucia responded, pleased that she'd caught enough of the conversation to understand what was happening. 'And, as the hostel is almost in the hospital grounds, you might like to do some patient visiting yourself.'

'Like you do?' Carol asked, looking very perky about the idea.

'Exactly! After all, you're the one who keeps telling me I should get about a bit more. And how can I go gadding about when I've all these lonely people tucked away in here with no friends or family near enough to call?'

'Gee, I'd love that,' Carol said, and Lucia stifled a momentary qualm about whether Carol's loquaciousness would appeal to everyone. 'They can always pretend they're asleep if they don't want to talk to me,' she added, and Lucia felt ashamed that her friend might have sensed her hesitation.

'Most people are delighted to have some company and often it's easier for them if the visitor does the talking because it saves them making that extra effort,' Lucia said quickly. 'I'll see you between now and Tuesday and, in the meantime, I'll have a chat to the people we've brought in who will be here long-term and see if they'd like you to visit them.'

As ever, she felt a surge of pride that she was part of the Service, and could legitimately say 'we've' brought in!

She said goodbye soon after and hurried up to the fifth floor where Lydia, an elderly woman from an aboriginal community in the far north-west of the state, was battling cancer.

'She's getting quieter and quieter,' the sister on duty whispered to Lucia as she walked into the small ward. 'And she didn't even object when Doctor suggested she might be more comfortable in the bed now.'

'Not a good sign,' Lucia agreed, walking back out to the corridor and down it to a small, single-bed room with windows facing west towards the green-clad mountains.

'Hello, Lydia,' she said quietly, and crossed the room to take the frail hand held out towards her. Through the papery skin she could feel bones, fragile as a bird's, clinging to hers with the last shreds of strength.

'It's been a lovely day,' she said quietly, 'hot but bright and sparkling—the way it is after a summer storm.'

The thin fingers tightened on hers for a moment. It was Lydia's only response these days—that and the hand stretched out to greet her, telling her she was still welcome.

Lucia sat beside the bed and spoke quietly, passing on the news about Carol and the accident and the new doctor. She was never sure what Lydia might want to know so she told her all the little snippets of things that had happened in her day.

But today it seemed different. As if Lydia, who usually lay and smiled at her while she talked, was not listening.

'Can I do something for you, Lydia?' she asked, when the woman's anxiety communicated itself to her more and more strongly. 'Is there someone you want to see? Your relatives, perhaps?'

The dark, wrinkled face, eyes deep-sunk with pain, moved slightly on the pillow.

'Something you want to ask the nurses?' Lucia guessed, but saw another negative response.

'The doctors?'

This time the frail claw responded, tightening into an almost painful grasp.

'The doctor here? Your specialist?'

Lydia's eyes filled with tears, and Lucia could feel her frustration at her inability to voice her needs.

Her other hand lifted off the bed cover and beckoned Lucia closer. She leaned over the bed, her head close to the woman's.

'Home!' The word grated out like a protest from a rusty gate hinge, and tears pricked behind Lucia's eyelids.

'Back to Coorawalla?' she whispered, the lovely name husky on her tongue. The answer was in the peace that spread across Lydia's face and in the bone-thin fingers that tightened and clung to her own.

'I'll speak to Dr Gregory tomorrow,' she promised. 'There's a clinic flight to the island on Wednesday. I can't promise anything, but. . .'

She knew Lydia would understand. When there was space on a flight the Service would happily take patients home, but they didn't have either staff or equipment to run a shuttle service for them.

Lydia nodded and closed her eyes and Lucia, reading the peace in her face, slipped quietly out of the room. One more visit and she was done. She wondered for a moment how Matt's accident patients were and whether they would be added to her visiting list in future.

Her final visit of the evening was to the men's medical ward where Gilbert Grace, a crotchety old prospector, was making life uncomfortable for staff and patients alike.

'Thought you'd forgotten me,' he growled, as she walked lightly towards his bed. 'Go and visit those wimmin before you visit me. Not important to you, am I?' It was his usual complaint, and Lucia supplied the answer he knew would come.

'I come to you last so I can spend more time with you. Besides,' she added, smiling cheekily at him, 'I don't want a goodnight kiss from ''wimmin''!'

She sat down beside his bed and opened the drawer in his bedside cabinet. The first time she'd visited Gilbert she'd brought a magazine about gemstones, hoping it might interest him to read about the geological processes that formed some of the beautiful minerals he collected.

'I don't bother with that reading stuff!' he'd snapped. 'Waste of time!' But she'd seen the way he had looked at the pictures and noticed the tenderness in his gnarled old hands as they rubbed across the dazzling colour photographs of amethyst and topaz.

'I could read it to you,' she'd suggested, and here she was, up to page forty-seven and still reading a few pages each evening.

'That young know-nothing reckons I can go back to the bush Friday.'

He interrupted a discourse on the origins of opal to impart this information, and Lucia knew that he would have had a reason to speak. She put down the book and looked at him, trying to guess whether he considered

this good or bad news. The 'young know-nothing' was
the very able registrar on the medical ward who had
been working with the specialist to discover an underlying cause for Gilbert's enlarged spleen.

Gilbert was a regular patient of the RFDS, turning
up at clinics in unexpected places but usually visiting
them at least three times a year. Jack said he came to
talk to other human beings when he tired of talking
to the trees!

'Does he think he's fixed the problem?' Lucia asked
cautiously, praying that her question would not prompt
one of Gilbert's colourful rages against the more con-
ventional members of the medical profession.

He had gone to the clinic to have an infected leg
wound treated and dressed, but Jack had been alarmed
at the profuse bleeding when he disturbed the surface
of the wound and had insisted on carrying out a full
examination of the independent old man. An enlarged
spleen had suggested underlying problems that required
further tests and Gilbert, protesting all the way but obviously sick enough to know he couldn't refuse help, had
been flown to the bay.

'Well, he says it ain't malaria and he knows another
twenty fancy things it also ain't, but if I keep taking
his tablets and see your lot a bit more regular I can live
with it, he reckons. He wanted to whip it out, you know,'
he continued in his confidential whisper that reached
into every corner of the ward. 'But I told him God
wouldn't have given me one just for him to take out.'

Lucia smiled.

'I'll finish the book before Friday,' she promised him,
and bent to give him the kiss on the cheek that was the
only physical contact he would permit.

She was smiling as she walked to the lift but her thoughts returned to Lydia, and a shadow of sorrow crept over her.

'It's almost as if she's decided to die,' she said to Matt as they strolled home through the darkened streets.

He had been waiting inside the main doors, and she knew that she had smiled too widely and walked too quickly towards him. Now she tried to ignore the feeling of lightness that swept her along beside him, and concentrated on her explanation.

'Six weeks ago, when the doctors suggested chemotherapy, she shifted happily into the hospital, moved the mattress onto the floor and sent her fluttering, wailing relatives away, saying she had "big business" to do and she didn't want them bothering her. Back then, she was going to fight. She demanded details of the weather every time I visited, as if the sultry monsoon season was helping her in some way or was tied to what she was doing.'

'Shifted her mattress onto the floor?' Matt asked, picking up on what was, to Lucia, the least important part of the story.

'Many of the older aboriginal people prefer to sleep on the floor. And that's another thing. Tonight the mattress was back on the bed.'

Matt heard the distress in Lucia's voice and touched her gently on the arm—one touch, that was all he would allow himself.

'I think some people decide they have had enough. As a doctor, I don't want to believe people can will themselves to die but I have seen people give up, as it were. But it isn't a harsh or chemically confused death,

Lucia, rather an acceptance of the pattern of things—an acknowledgement of the way things were meant to be.'

'As if we all have some allotted span of time on earth, and once that time is up we should give in gracefully?'

He heard the disbelief in her voice and, beyond that, the strain he had seen for an instant earlier—when he'd spoken of medical careers.

'Could a doctor ever agree with that?' he joked, hoping to defuse a situation he didn't understand. 'Aren't we medical men put on earth with the God-given, state-approved right to save lives?' He stood still, turned towards her and smiled.

'And isn't this exceptional evening, with a star-filled sky above us and the lapping of the water on a beach not far away, too beautiful for such philosophical discussions? Your friend's beliefs might make her death not only a release from pain but be a gateway, in her mind, to something even better beyond. She is peaceful and at ease, you say, or will be once we take her home.'

In the light from the now-risen moon he saw the frown ease away from between her eyes and her lips parted, stretching their fullness into a breath-taking smile.

'Of course, you're right,' she whispered. 'She must have decided to give white man's medicine a go originally, or she wouldn't have agreed to come to town. I know they finished the second course of chemo a fortnight ago. I suppose if she knew within herself she wasn't any better, she might have begun to look to the future and turned back to her own beliefs.'

'I think you could be right,' he whispered, 'as well as very beautiful!'

Forgetting his promise to keep physical contact to a

minimum, he lifted his hand and, with the tip of his little finger, he traced the firm, clear edge of her profile then returned from the small, neat chin and followed the outline of the lovely lips, feeling them quiver beneath his touch.

Lucia froze, outwardly immobile but inwardly a churning restlessness began that built and built until she had to bite her lip to stop herself from crying out when his finger ceased its tender exploration.

'I think we should keep walking,' he muttered, grasping her elbow without a semblance of his earlier gentleness and propelling her at a smart pace along the footpath.

I wanted him to kiss me, she realised as she lengthened her stride to keep up with him. Yet the disappointment blended with the excitement his firm asexual grasp was generating in her nervous system, making a potent cocktail of untested emotions.

'We don't have to run,' she objected, pleased that she could still make light of an unnerving situation.

'I'm sorry,' he apologised, slowing his pace immediately. 'I don't usually behave like this. Must be the first day back at work or the tropical air or the unexpected rescue flight. I seem to have lost all my balance.'

So it's not me at all, Lucia thought, considerably put out by the string of excuses he'd offered. She walked along in silence, still enjoying whatever it was that made her feel. . .uncomfortable in some ways, yes, but. . .content, that was it, in this man's company. And I wouldn't tell him that it was him making me feel a bit strange either, she reminded herself. Not yet, definitely.

But would she ever?

'Have we passed your house?' she asked as they

stopped at her aunt's gate for the second time that day. 'You didn't have to see me to the door. Rainbow Bay is just a grown-up fishing village. Practically crime-free.'

He was so close she thought a deep breath might cause their chests to meet, and she fancied that she could feel the heat of his body radiating out towards her skin.

'It is my pleasure to see you safely home,' he assured her. 'Anyway, my flat is at the back of number sixty-four, four houses closer to the base.'

In the darkness his accent sounded stronger and Lucia suddenly thought of a thousand things she wanted to know about him; about his home, and family, and friends, and ambitions and. . .dreams?

'I will see you tomorrow,' she said, fighting down a desire to ask him in for a cup of coffee. In the four months she'd lived with Aunt Steph she'd never invited anyone in for coffee. To set a precedent now would invite questions, and she didn't know the answers to the kind of questions her aunt would ask.

'In the morning,' he stressed. She felt him take her hand, and before she realised what he was doing he had raised it to his lips and was pressing a kiss into her so-sensitive palm.

His lips teased and tickled at her skin but the fire they started soon burnt away any feeling of strangeness and, as he closed her fingers over his kiss, she felt a trembling begin in her toes and work its way up through her body.

'*À demain*,' he said and the words, familiar from school lessons, had a throaty significance that stirred the strange turbulence within her to a fever-ish madness.

'*À demain*,' she echoed experimentally, testing the strangeness against her tongue, then she turned and raced up the stairs, her heart keeping pace with her flying feet.

CHAPTER FOUR

Lucia walked slowly down the street next morning, trying not to look too interested as she passed number sixty-four. She was early for work so she could dawdle along. If he hadn't already left, he might catch up with her. The summer sun was warm, but not yet burning in intensity, and she felt it melt into her skin, filling her with a sense of well-being.

Not that it had anything to do with Matt Laurant, she assured herself. And nor did she care if he caught up with her or not. He was just passing through and while he might want a girlfriend for the twelve months he would be with the Service she didn't think she was a twelve-month kind of person.

'And what's your programme for today?'

His voice brought her to a halt and he came level in two strides. He was thinking of work and she was thinking of relationships! She smiled at her wayward thoughts and they moved off towards the base, falling easily into step as if walking together was something they'd practised.

'I must speak to Jack about Lydia going home,' she told him. 'Gilbert, one of our other patients, is also due for discharge but the hospital will make his discharge arrangements. I don't think Lydia has told her doctor she wants to go. In that case, it will be up to Jack to smooth out any problems.'

'So it's not fly them in then forget them at all,' Matt

pointed out, smiling at her in a way that made the sun seem warmer, the sky bluer and the day brighter. 'You can handle discharges as well as follow-up work if it is necessary.'

He seemed pleased by this and Lucia felt an equal pleasure—that he would care what happened to their patients and not simply look at his time with the Flying Doctors as a job that promised a measure of excitement.

'Our accident cases are different,' she explained, 'because they are often travellers passing through our area. Most of the time they are transferred to hospitals closer to their homes as soon as they are well enough to make the journey. But for many of the people in isolated places our doctors are their local GPs, remember. So of course we must know about discharges, and our doctors must work with the local specialists and the hospital staff to arrange follow-up treatment and consultations.'

'You are very passionate about it,' he teased, and heard her sigh.

'Once,' she told him, stopping and turning to look into his face as if willing him to understand what she was about to say. 'Once,' she repeated, 'I thought it would be my life's work. It was a dream I'd had—we'd had!'

We'd had? Lucia and a friend? A male friend, perhaps? The thought upset him and he moved on again, saying, 'One day you might tell me about it,' in a strained voice he barely recognised as his own.

'One day, maybe I will,' she replied, but he heard so much doubt in her voice that he wondered if she would.

'Morning, you two! Heard the news?'

Susan was shutting her car door as they turned into the base gardens.

'No!' Lucia groaned, knowing it wouldn't be good.

'What news?' Matt asked, the excitement he seemed to relish already shining in his eyes.

'There was a fire on a trawler. The two crew tried to put it out, getting themselves burnt in the process. They were thrown into the water when the fuel tank exploded, so they added near-drowning and a touch of hypothermia to their ills.'

Lucia smiled. Susan always described patients with a degree of exasperation, as if they had deliberately sought trouble to inconvenience the Service. Yet she was the most popular of all the flight nurses, not only because of her long service but also because the outback people liked her matter-of-fact manner and her practical 'Let's get on with the job' attitude.

'So what has happened to these men?' Matt asked, walking with the two women towards the front door. 'Where are they now?'

'Almost at the hospital,' Susan told him. 'Another boat picked them up—lucky for them they were fishing in a group—and took them to Coorawalla. Eddie's was the closest plane, so he and the locum flew across there and collected them. They were due to land at the Bay airport about half an hour ago.'

'And will Eddie now fly back to wherever he was to continue the clinic flight?' Matt asked, and Lucia smiled sympathetically at him. It was hard for newcomers to remember all the names—especially the strange-sounding Aboriginal ones—but before she could explain Susan was speaking again.

'Eddie can't go back,' she said with a certain degree

of satisfaction. 'Allysha will fly the locum back to Caltura, where they'll pick up Christa before flying on to "Rosemount" and Cameron River for the last two clinics.'

'Eddie can't go back but the locum can?' Matt asked, and this time Lucia came to his rescue.

'Doctors and nursing staff can work unlimited hours,' she explained. 'Usually they are on call for twenty-four hour shifts so, even if they have been up all night with an emergency, they can still be called out during the day. Once you start on roster you'll learn to sleep standing up.'

'I learnt that during my first two years in hospitals,' he assured her. 'I am certain the art of it will come back to me! But Eddie?'

'Pilots are restricted to twelve hours' flying in any twenty-four-hour period. When Eddie flew from Rainbow Bay to Caltura, then on to Coorawalla and back to Rainbow Bay it must have brought him up to the limit or close enough that another day's flying is impossible.'

They had paused outside the main doors, and Lucia saw Matt smile cheekily.

'He could not fly halfway back to the place with the wild-sounding name, then say, "That's it for me for today," and give up controls of his plane—that I *do* understand! And nor would I want him going to sleep while he was flying me somewhere.'

Susan chuckled and led the way through the door.

'But what does it mean to us here at the base? Will rosters be changed?' Matt asked Lucia, waving her through ahead of him.

'In this case I wouldn't think so,' she replied. 'If the

locum had not been able to return to the clinic run for
some reason the next doctor on call would have gone
in his place.'

She grinned at him. 'Looks like you'll have to wait
until Thursday, after all. That's your first rostered
clinic.'

'Don't remind me!' he joked. 'I'm terrified just thinking about it.'

Lucia sensed truth behind the lightly spoken words
and reached out, touching him fleetingly on the arm.

'Susan will look after you,' she reassured him. 'She
could run the clinics single-handed.' She smiled up at
him and added, 'They only take you doctors along to
sign the prescriptions!'

As he smiled back a warm glow filled her body and
she said, 'See you later,' in a breathless little voice, and
whisked herself away into the safety of Leonie's office.

'You might take over Lucia's job today and phone
the hospital for a follow-up on those two chaps we
brought in yesterday. I'd like to know what their actual
injuries were.'

Jack Gregory's voice made Matt realise that he was
standing in the foyer like a misplaced statue.

'I'd be happy to do that,' he replied. 'I visited the
two men yesterday evening but the doctors who had
treated them were off duty at the time.'

'Lucia's our most regular hospital visitor,' Jack said,
and Matt thought he saw a twinkle in the older man's
green eyes.

'Yes, I walked up with her,' Matt explained rather
stiffly, not wanting Jack to think that he was hiding
anything. 'She has a kind heart to do the visiting,' he
added, and hoped that he hadn't given away the regard

he already felt for the lovely young woman.

'She has, indeed,' Jack ageed. 'Kind enough, I'm sure, to show you where we keep the hospitalised patient files. Once you get through to that stay-at-home lot up there you might as well check on our other charges. It will give you some idea of the diversity of our work.'

Matt nodded, unwilling to reveal any more by telling Jack that Lucia had already filled him in on the patients.

He walked across to the desk he had been given— the absent locum's desk. Before that it had belonged to James and before him, who knew? How many doctors had sat here like he was now, feeling alone and uncertain but incredibly excited to be part of something so unique?

'Jack asked me to bring you these files.'

Not totally alone, he realised, looking up into Lucia's smiling face.

'I didn't bring Lydia's,' she went on to explain. 'I told Jack she wanted to go home, so he took her file and will contact her specialist himself.'

She hesitated and he saw the golden skin on her forehead wrinkle into a puzzled frown.

'Jack made it sound as if he might have trouble arranging for her to be discharged. Wouldn't you think, once the doctor knows that's what she wants, it would be easy?'

He pushed the files to one corner of his desk and propped his chin on his hands as he looked up at her.

'It should be,' he said gently. 'But doctors are just ordinary people, you know. Just as you get some men of any trade talking as if they know everything, some doctors think they know all the answers. Others can feel as jealous of a patient as they are of their wives and sweethearts. It's human nature.'

'It's stupidity!' Lucia said. 'Doctors are supposed to be intelligent and well educated. They should put the patient first.'

He smiled at her disapproval.

'Most of them do,' he assured her. 'But the man Jack has to speak to about your friend, Lydia, may have excellent medical reasons for wanting to keep her in hospital.'

I love it when he smiles like that. The thought flashed like a swift across her mind and she blushed, stammered incoherently about filing, and fled.

I really must pull myself together, she scolded herself, hurrying to the kitchen to make coffee for Leonie. If I start mooning around the office Dr Flint will be the first to spot it and he'll tease me to death and embarrass Matt unbearably.

She straightened up, the thought of Matt's embarrassment a sufficient goad to hide the strangeness his presence was causing to her innermost being.

Matt watched her go and dragged his mind away from the memory of the feel of her, the warmth and softness of her skin and the hesitancy in her breathing when he had folded her fingers over his kiss.

She is not a girl to love and leave, he warned himself, then he pulled the top file towards him and opened it.

Karl Roberts was the name of the pilot they had cut out of the plane. He had been sleeping when Matt had visited the hospital but a glance at the man's casts, and the chart at the end of the bed, had confirmed the knee fracture Jack had suspected, left tib and fib, and damage to sinews and tendons of both ankles.

He read through the file, amazed at the clinical detail Jack had amassed even at the site of the accident. I must consider it a patient file like any patient file, he reminded himself, wherever I might be treating the sick or injured person.

He picked up the phone and was fortunate enough to get straight onto the orthopaedic registrar who had treated both men.

'We did an open reduction on Roberts's knee,' the doctor told him. 'Our duty surgeon and local microspecialist fixed the leg wound—enough arterial damage to warrant a graft—and, naturally, we're watching for signs of fat embolisms. He'd lost a lot of blood by the time we saw him, but once we started him on full blood he picked up all right. I'll get someone to photocopy our files and fax them off to you later today.'

'And the passenger?' Matt opened the next file. 'Alan Wilmott?' He had spoken to Alan the previous evening and although his leg, strung up in traction, was paining him Matt was certain that he would be all right.

'Concussed, according to your files and our observations, for close to four hours. Even if his leg wasn't busted we'd have kept him in for observation. Of course he's conscious now, but can't remember anything immediately preceding the crash. Must have bumped his head as they landed and not when they went into the ditch Jack described in his accident report.'

Accident report? Matt turned back to the first file and leafed through it until he found the sheet with that heading. He skimmed through it while he listened to the doctor explain further. 'As far as he's concerned, one minute they were flying happily through blue sky and the next he was in hospital. You can imagine how happy that's making the air safety boys who've been trying to question him.'

'There will be an investigation?' Matt asked, wondering about the jobs of men who had to make their way to out-of-the-way places and try to piece together why a plane had crashed. Everything he learned was adding new dimensions to his concept of this foreign country.

'Of course. There are more rules about planes and pilots than there are about us doctors practising,' the man said, almost repeating what Susan and Lucia had told him earlier. 'Now, do you want any other info from up here? Shall I transfer you through to another ward?'

Matt looked at the files and refused the offer, wanting to read through the patients' details before he spoke to the men or women who were treating them at the moment.

He studied Carol Benson's first, seeing the neat follow-up information Lucia had obviously printed in—far easier to read than the medical illegibility higher up the page!

Lucia! An image of her dark shining hair, her lustrous eyes and shy yet provocative smile flicked into his mind and he shut his eyes to stop her intruding.

Carol Benson's file repeated what Lucia had told him about the woman but he saw the note that read 'Phaeochromocytoma' and smiled to himself. He'd known there was something rare that could present as pre-eclampsia! Lifting the phone, he called the obstetrics ward.

'You'll note her blood pressure was peaking to unsafe levels when she first came in and I felt we had to use a background hypertensive. I decided on methyldopa.' The speaker was a woman, which surprised him. In his experience women specialists in O and G were fairly rare.

'Of all the available drugs, it's the one which has had the most long-term follow-up tests on children exposed to it *in utero* and no complications have yet been found,' the confident voice continued. 'I gave Lucia the details for your files but, from memory, we began with a loading dose of 750 mg. She's onto 250 mg four times a day now but I want to monitor her at that level for at least a week before I discharge her to a hostel.'

'And when she is in the hostel, who will be her doctor?' Matt asked.

'Oh, she'll still see me regularly. I do out-patient clinics and the hostel is just beyond the hospital grounds, so she will not be far away from specialist care. Pop in yourself some time,' she suggested, 'and meet some of the staff.'

'I will do that,' Matt promised, then asked to be transferred to Men's Medical.

'I'm sorry, but Sister and Dr Evans are doing their round,' a young nurse told him in a voice that said it was more than her life was worth to interrupt them. 'I know Mr Grace is due for discharge so Doctor will be ringing you people to talk about the possibility of transport for him some time soon.'

Matt thanked her and hung up. Getting onto two out of the three people he wanted was enough luck for one day. No longer unwilling to be distracted, he thought of Lucia again. If she visited the hospital every night when did she go out with her boyfriend? Hope flickered to life. Maybe she didn't have one. Maybe he could ask her out but keep it light—a friendship.

'Hi! If you've finished with the files I'm to talk to you about clinics.'

He looked up to see the handsome man who had

introduced himself the day before as Peter Flint.

'You are here today?' he asked politely, remembering the man's joking remark.

Peter grinned, a quick flash of white teeth and an added sparkle in his eyes.

'I'm here, but Jack isn't,' he explained. 'Not that he ever spends his off-duty days at home. The man's a workaholic and you'll have to watch him or he'll turn you into one as well. Now, I'll show you the map of the area we cover and explain the clinic runs and then, out of the goodness of my heart, I'll take you up to the hospital for a canteen lunch. It's a good way to meet the staff you'll be talking to on the phone, not to mention some of the loveliest nurses under this tropical sun.'

Matt found himself swept along by Peter's enthusiasm. Maybe women would object to a hint of chauvinism in his delight but Matt suspected it was more his speech pattern and natural exuberance. He followed him into the radio room and was formally introduced to Katie, who looked up from her computer screen, smiled and nodded and turned away to answer one of the bank of phones on her desk.

'These maps show it best,' Peter explained, spreading out a map of the northern area of the state. 'Different colours are for different days, dotted lines show fortnightly clinic flights, uninterrupted lines are weekly and these dashes in blue are a monthly Friday clinic we do to three properties and an outlying island in the far north.'

The excitement that was never far away bubbled up again, and Matt became absorbed in the details Peter was explaining. So absorbed that he was startled when Peter said, 'Well, that's it! You'll understand it better once you've actually flown a regular clinic trip. Now, my car's out the back so let's go and see how many of the female medical population of Rainbow Bay are just dying to meet a handsome young French doctor.'

'We should tell someone? Say where we are going, or goodbye?' Matt asked, not certain whether he wanted to be swept along in the wake of Peter's goodwill.

'If you want to say goodbye to someone say "Goodbye, Katie" to our lovely radio operator, and move. Even though he's not officially here, Jack will notice if we're late back and as for Leonie! That woman eats doctor's bones for breakfast, I swear!'

Matt followed him, chuckling at the image of the very proper Mrs Cooper gnawing on a femur.

'You can laugh now,' Peter warned, leading him out into the bright sunshine that pressed heat into the paved car park, 'but you wait until you forget to fill in a requisition or don't sign the prescription order that's sent to Brisbane to replenish medical chest supplies. It'll be your bones she gnaws, my lad!'

Peter opened the passenger door of a sporty red car and ushered him in, but as he slid into the hot, stuffy interior Matt felt a momentary pang of regret. He'd have liked to have told Lucia where he was going; to have said goodbye to her, as well as to Katie!

Lucia watched them go from the lunch-room window, sadness etching her heart with the bitter bite of acid. Peter would introduce Matt to all the prettiest nurses at the hospital. She had heard that it was his way of welcoming all the new single men who joined the staff.

'I don't think he does it out of kindness.' Katie's voice sounded right behind her and Lucia saw that she, too, was watching the car drive away. 'I think it gives him an excuse to look over any new ''talent'' at the hospital.'

'That's not a very nice thing to say—about Peter or the staff at the hospital,' Lucia protested. Katie's grim look disappeared, and she smiled.

'You are too nice to be real!' she said, shaking her head in mock reproof. 'Peter Flint teases you unmercifully and makes the most sexist remarks to you and here you are, defending him.'

'Well, maybe he's not very happy deep down and that's why he makes a joke of everything and plays around, hoping he might one day find something he knows is missing from his life but can't quite identify.'

'Pollyanna now!' Katie scoffed. 'I'd like to think you might be right, but you're more likely to find that Peter Flint is one of those golden people who breeze through life having a fabulous time because they are so secure in their own wonderfulness!'

And on that tart note she stomped out of the room, leaving Lucia staring, open-mouthed, after her.

She thought about the words while she made herself a cup of coffee, then said, 'She can't be right,' to the empty room and settled down to eat her sandwiches, trying not to think about Matt Laurant sitting at a table simply cluttered with beautiful blondes twenty minutes' walk away.

It was only natural that he should want to meet some other young people, she told herself. He'll be here for a year and will need friends to visit on days off, people with whom he can relax—a girlfriend! Her mind faltered over the last thought. Peter always had a string of women fluttering about him—calling him at work, driving his car and crowding around him at base barbecues and staff parties. And Matt was every bit as good-looking as Peter—in a different, less flamboyant way, of course.

'We'll take your friend, Lydia, home on Wednesday.' Jack interrupted her thoughts as he came in and reached for his favourite coffee-mug. 'She was keen to have treatment when she first came to town, wasn't she?'

Lucia frowned at him. He sounded uncertain of himself, which was as unlikely as finding Peter without a girlfriend. She waited until he had fished a packet of sandwiches out of the refrigerator and sat down opposite her before she answered.

'Very keen,' she said firmly. 'Some of the patients I've visited are excited about being in hospital because it's the first time in their lives anyone has made a fuss of them, but with Lydia it was different. She was a wise woman among her own people and knew about natural drugs and remedies. I think she considered chemo-therapy a challenge—a kind of "let's see what white man's medicine can do".'

Jack smiled at her.

'Well, thank you for that insight, Lucia,' he said, his green eyes twinkling into hers. 'I worry sometimes that we might unknowingly pressure people into coming to town. Because they don't have the convenience of a hospital or GP nearby, do we tend to over-persuade them?'

Lucia heard the door open behind her, and turned to see Susan come in.

'Over-persuade them?' she said, joining in the conversation in her usual forthright manner. 'Most people are only too glad to be closer to medical help if there's the slightest doubt that whatever ails them is likely to get worse. I have more problem persuading people they needn't come than pressuring people who should.'

'Now, there's a second vote of confidence! Thanks, Susan,' Jack said, scrunching the plastic wrap into a tiny ball and firing it at the rubbish bin. 'I think a day without an emergency call must be affecting my nerves. I don't like it when things are too quiet.'

'Don't ever say that!' Susan warned. 'Next thing you know Katie will be pressing the alarm, we'll all rush into the radio room and it will be on again.'

'Without me,' Jack reminded her. 'Peter's on duty and on call tonight. Any emergency is his baby.'

He rose and stretched then walked towards the door, pausing to touch Lucia on the top of her head.

'Wise child!' he murmured, and then he was gone.

'Wise child indeed!' Susan retorted when the door had shut behind him. 'Why did you let Peter Flint take your young man along to the hospital? You know he'll introduce him to every unattached woman on the staff up there.'

Lucia felt colour rush into her cheeks.

'He's not my young man!' she told Susan, hoping that her voice wasn't shaking as much as her intestines. 'I'm practically engaged to Anthony back home.'

'No one who's ''practically engaged'' spends her weekends cooking for her aunt and visiting people at the hospital. If you're ''practically engaged'' to this fellow why did you leave home and why doesn't he visit you at weekends—take you out, give you a bit of pleasure and company?'

Could her cheeks get any hotter? She pressed her hands against them but couldn't think of a satisfactory reply to any of Susan's questions.

'We sort of grew up together,' she muttered. 'His brother, Daniel, and Anthony and I.' She hesitated, probing her thoughts as if testing an inner bruise. No, she was not ready yet to talk about Daniel. 'We kind of drifted into it going about a bit together,' she added. 'It's more an expectation than an engagement.'

'An expectation that one day, completely out of the blue, you might fall in love with each other? Wake up, Lucia. If it hasn't already happened it's not likely to happen now—especially if you never see the guy. Go out with Matt. Enjoy yourself a little.'

'But he's only here for a year. He'll be going home to France!'

It might as well be to the moon, her voice intimated.

Susan laughed. 'I've been there, dear,' she said, still smiling. 'It's really very civilised, and the French would be offended at you making it sound like the North Pole or somewhere equally remote.'

Lucia shook her head. 'I didn't mean that,' she protested. 'I meant he's only here for a short time so our friendship couldn't lead anywhere.'

'Nonsense, you ridiculous child! There are a lot of places a friendship could lead in a week, let alone a year! He seems a polite, sensible young man. If I had a daughter I'd be pleased to see her going out with someone half as nice—not to mention good-looking!'

'He is good-looking, isn't he?' Lucia mused, then roused herself from sliding back into a daydream and said abruptly, 'But he hasn't asked me out, anyway, and there's no reason why he should.'

But Susan only laughed and shook her head, and carried her coffee out of the room.

Left on her own, Lucia wondered for a moment what

she would say if the unlikely did happen and Matt asked
her to go out with him but, after considering and dis-
carding several possible replies, she decided that she
had no idea how she would react, and tidied up the
lunch-room before going back to work.

'Are you packing the clinic files for Coorawalla?'
Leonie asked, reminding her in the nicest possible way
that it was now her job to see the files were in the case
that went on the clinic plane.

'I'm going through them now. Jane's doing immunis-
ations so she asked me to check all the children's dates
and see who's due for what.'

Leonie nodded.

'Jack suggested she do tetanus, too,' Leonie told
her. 'Very few adults think about tetanus boosters until
they cut themselves and need a shot and in places like
Coorawalla, where there's no hospital, he's concerned
it could be too late by the time we get there. People
should have boosters every ten years.'

'I can look through the files for those who haven't
had recent boosters and give Jane a list. The problem
is that the people probably won't turn up at the clinic
unless there's something else wrong with them.'

'Don't you believe it,' Leonie said with a smile. 'With
Lydia returning home, it will be a grand social occasion
at Coorawalla. That's why Jack suggested taking extra
vaccine on this visit.'

It was Lucia's turn to smile as she thought of all the
unsuspecting people arriving at the airstrip to welcome
Lydia home, only to find Peter and Jane lining them up
for tetanus boosters. She carried the Coorawalla files
across to her desk and began to go through them.

Once she had checked the vaccinations she would

give the files and her own lists to Jane, who would read through them once more to check on ongoing treatments that might require special or extra drugs. Jane would also look for updated entries which would show that a radio consultation had taken place since their last clinic visit.

The last person to read the files would be the clinic doctor, and he usually spent the flight time familiarising himself with the patients he was about to see.

To outsiders it might seem a clumsy system, but Lucia knew that it worked and worked well. She wondered what Matt would think of it all, once he became a 'working part' of the Flying Doctors' widespread mantle of safety.

CHAPTER FIVE

MATT spent the afternoon with Peter, listening in to the phone consultations which were such an important part of the service.

'If you go through to the equipment room you'll find a medical chest,' Peter told him. 'Carry it in here and have a look at its contents while I talk—that way you'll see what the people at the other end will be doing while I speak to them.'

Lucia was in the corridor outside the radio room and gave Matt a slightly wary smile. For a moment he wanted to linger with her; to make her smile properly so that he could see the sparkle light up her eyes.

'Peter's sent me to find a medical chest,' he explained, trying to banish the image of sparkling eyes.

'I'll show you where it is,' she said quietly, and turned to lead him into the equipment room.

She was so close that he could smell a soft perfume rising from her riot of dusky curls, and he felt a stirring that all Peter's lovely nursing friends had failed to prompt.

'There,' she said, her voice husky as if their closeness was affecting her as badly as it was affecting him.

'Thank you, Lucia,' he whispered, stiffening every sinew in his body to prevent himself from leaning forward and kissing her, just once, on her soft, full, pale pink lips. But his control failed and his head, of its own volition, tilted forward. Holding his breath, lest escaping air break the magic spell, he touched his lips to hers, tasting the honeyed sweetness of that tempting mouth— tasting its freshness, its innocence.

When he raised his head she hesitated for a moment, as if held by the tension in his body, then slipped away from him, her footsteps echoing down the corridor as she returned to whatever task he had interrupted. He groaned and leant his head against the cool metal of the tiered shelving.

'Imbecile!' he muttered at himself. 'Second day at work and you are making a nuisance of yourself with a girl in the equipment room!'

He reached up and wrestled the chest off the shelf, then lugged it back into the radio room. Putting aside all thoughts of Lucia, he opened it and his mind was immediately diverted as he sorted through the layered contents. Everything from bandages and safety pins to prescription drugs.

So that explains Bill having morphine sulphate to give the injured pilot! And, because it could be given subcutaneously or intramuscularly, a layman could administer it in an emergency.

Studying the list of contents fixed in the top of the chest, he wondered at the forethought that had provided isolated people with the wherewithal to save their own or another person's life. He was still reading through the list when he heard Peter greet a caller, his voice deep and full of a calming certainty that impressed Matt immensely.

This was a different man to the outrageous playboy he'd seen in action over lunch!

'What has he been doing this morning, Mrs Cranston?' Peter asked, cutting through a litany of symptoms that Matt could hear from where he sat. While he listened Peter was bringing up the patient's name on the computer and checking through the file notes, his finger pausing every now and then as he mentally computed what the abbreviated information was telling him.

'Working in the shed?'

'That's helpful,' Peter muttered in an aside to Matt, shifting the phone out a small distance from his ear so that Matt could hear the conversation more clearly.

'I need to know what he was doing in the shed,' he explained. 'If he was mixing chemicals for spraying a little of it could have splashed into his eye. If he was fixing machinery and using a grinder, then it might be a bit of metal in there. Do you think you could put down the phone and go and ask him?' he continued quietly and as the phone clattered onto a bench or table, Peter turned to Matt again.

'What do you think?' he asked.

Matt smiled at him.

'I'm not entirely stupid,' he said. 'I'm not thinking anything until I hear more. Has she flushed the eye with water?'

'He did that as soon as he came in at lunchtime, she said. Held his head under the kitchen tap and ran water into it for ten minutes, but she was getting the kids' lunch and cooking cakes for an Election Day stall at the local community hall and she didn't think to ask him what had happened.'

'So if it was sore at lunchtime, why ring now? It's nearly four o'clock.'

Now Peter smiled.

'He flushed it out at lunchtime but we don't know that it was sore then,' he reminded Matt. 'He went off

to have a sleep after lunch and woke up in agony. I'm
certain, above her talking, that I could hear the man
moaning so it's bad.'

Matt looked at Peter, sure that the other doctor had
already guessed at a probable diagnosis, and then they
heard Mrs Cranston lift the phone.

'He was welding a new gate early this morning, he
took it out to the paddock and slipped it onto the old
hinge,' she said, and Peter nodded and smiled.

'He's got a welding flash, Mrs Cranston. He either
wasn't using his mask or he slipped it to one side to
look at something and the burn caught him. Is it one
eye or both?'

Matt missed the reply but saw Peter's finger run down
a blue chart on the desk in front of him.

'You'll need Item Number 164, Mrs Cranston,' he
said. 'It's on tray A but it should be refrigerated. Do
you keep the R items in the fridge?'

She must have assented for Peter said, 'That's great.
Now, each container has a single dose. You use it just
like ordinary eyedrops, so hold his eyelids open and
drop it in. It will anaesthetise the eye and stop the
excruciating pain for a short time.'

Peter paused for a moment and Matt realised that the
woman would be writing down his instructions.

'On Tray A, Item 204, you'll find eyepads. Tape one
lightly over his eye when you've finished, then give
him some Panadeine or other painkiller that can begin
working while the eye's anaesthetised. The anaesthetic
effect will probably only last about half an hour to an
hour. You might assure him that the intensity of the
pain does wear off but if it's still severe in an hour
ring me again. We can give him another dose of the

Amethocaine but you'd better talk to me first.'

Again he paused but this time he wrote down the instructions he had given onto a patient file sheet, then typed the date, time and medication into the computer.

'Now, you'd better read back the instructions,' he suggested, 'so we both know what we're doing.'

Matt was impressed by this casual approach, aware that Peter was making certain that Mrs Cranston understood what she was to do without undermining her confidence.

'Great! Now, ring me in an hour whatever happens,' he reminded her, added, 'Good luck,' and hung up.

'See how easy it is?' He turned to Matt with a grin.

'Easy if you know the people. A flash from an electric welder? It's not exactly a common GP problem, is it?' Matt retorted.

'Common enough up here. It's like a superficial burn to the surface of the cornea,' Peter told him. 'Suspect it when the pain doesn't start till later—usually six to twelve hours later. Most of the poor blighters don't realise there's anything wrong until they wake in agony at two in the morning. All we can do is anaesthetise it and suggest painkillers. The pain will eventually wear off.'

'And all that paperwork and computer work you did?' Matt asked, wondering why so many records needed to be kept.

'Sometimes I think it's a plot to keep us busy,' Peter complained. 'We have to log all our consultations in a day book—that's the equivalent of an appointment book in a regular surgery. We need the patient's file—if he or she is a regular—at hand so we know things like drug allergies, regularly prescribed medication and the general state of the patient's health.'

'So a persistent cough in a child with no history of asthma may be just that, while a persistent cough in an asthmatic could be a precursor for a bad attack?'

'Exactly,' Peter replied. 'And having the file to hand also means we can write in what we've done, how we've treated the patient and, later on, any follow-up details.'

Matt nodded his understanding.

'And the computer?' he asked. 'Surely that is duplicating the work you are dong on the written files.'

'Duplicating?' Peter shrieked, throwing his arms into the air in despair. 'As far as I'm concerned it's quadrupling it, but I must admit I am computer illiterate and the things terrify me! I know how to access files, type in information and save and that's the limit of my ability. Whenever any glitch appears every member of this staff accuses me of causing it, although, I swear to you, I don't even walk past a computer if I can avoid it.'

'Why use it, then?' Matt asked, after a quiet chuckle at Peter's admission.

'Because we have to,' Peter told him. 'And, to be honest, I can see the point. Eventually, we'll all be swooping through the ether with our little laptops tucked into our medical bags instead of bulky cases of patient files. We'll have ducky little modems and terminals at our clinic stops and will be able to call up all manner of information that should be lurking somewhere in our overloaded brains.'

'As a reference tool I can see its value, but will there ever be a time when computers are so reliable they will do away with hard copies of files and records?' Matt argued. 'What if you get to one of those far-off places and your computer battery is flat, or you hook up to local generated power and blow its memory?'

Peter looked at him, a gleam of appreciation in his blue eyes.

'I must remember that for my next argument with Jack,' he said warmly. 'Welcome aboard, Matt Laurant! I did wonder about you when you showed less than ecstatic appreciation of my efforts on your behalf at lunchtime, but if you're another anti-computers-taking-over-the-world person I know we'll become firm friends.'

He clapped Matt on the shoulder, then turned away as the shrilling of the phone demanded his attention.

Matt sat and listened while Peter reassured a nervous new mother that her baby probably didn't have anything seriously wrong because it had failed to pass a bowel motion at the regular time that day.

'What a difference the phone must make to these women,' Matt remarked, while Peter wrote his notes.

'Good in some ways and not so good in others,' Peter told him. 'If that woman had still been on a radio link, she would probably have aired her concerns over the radio and fifteen women could all have given her reassurance, remedies and stories of how many days their infants went without a bowel motion. Now she has my professional assurance but none of the "folklore" or "bush remedy" stuff that was passed around in the radio days.'

'I see what you mean. The radio for those women was a link with other women—their equivalent of sitting in the waiting-room at the baby health clinic or meeting other women at the local shopping centre.'

Peter nodded.

'It gave them the opportunity to talk to neighbours;

to gossip over the back fence, even though the back fence might be fifty miles away.'

Matt was surprised by the depth of understanding he heard in Peter's voice. This empathy with women seemed strangely at odds with his behaviour towards them. Oh, he was charming enough in their company but he gave the impression that, to him, they were delightful playthings to be admired, teased, praised, cajoled—and probably taken to bed—but definitely not to be taken seriously!

'There's a young woman on the radio, Peter.' Katie's voice interrupted Matt's thoughts.

'She's travelling north-west on a camping trip with six others in a minibus and complaining, with a great deal of ums and ahs and obvious embarrassment, about frequency and a burning pain on urination.'

The radio officer stood up from her chair.

'You can take it here but don't you tease her. The poor thing's mortified at having to yell all this into the handset as it is. Don't make it any worse for her.'

Matt saw Peter frown as he moved across to Katie's chair. Had her comment annoyed him? He didn't know Peter well and before he'd heard him speak about the isolation of the women in their 'practice' he might have suspected he could be flippant in such a situation. But Katie should know him better. Lucia had told him they'd both worked here for some years.

He heard Peter introduce himself and ask for the woman's name, home address and present whereabouts.

'Now, I'll ask you questions and all you need do is answer yes or no,' Peter explained. 'Will this worry you? Do you want to ask your friends to move away so you'll be more private?'

'Just when I'm so mad at him I could kill him, he does something understanding like that,' Katie muttered, and stalked out of the room.

Matt listened as Peter ran through the symptoms of cystitis, wondering if travellers also carried comprehensive drug chests and if not how Peter was going to manage this problem.

'OK,' Peter said at last. 'Now it's your turn to tell me things. What antibiotics are you carrying in your first-aid kit?'

There was a pause and Matt decided that she must be asking someone to check.

'Bactrim, Eryc, Augmentin and Amoxil—that's some collection,' Peter remarked, then listened while the woman explained that they had all gone to their GPs before embarking on their adventure and each had been given a different prescription.

'Which is yours?'

The reply, 'Amoxil,' reached Matt quite clearly.

'So, if your doctor prescribed it, can I assume you have had it before and are not allergic to it?' Peter asked.

'OK,' he told her, after listening to a list of the infections her doctor had cured with Amoxil, 'start on it now. What strength are the tablets?'

Again there was a pause before she reported they were capsules, 250 mg each.

'Take one every eight hours,' Peter told her, adding warningly, 'and I mean eight hours. Set an alarm to wake yourself in the night. It's important the medication stays in the bloodstream.'

He paused for a moment and added, 'Would you have any bicarb soda with you?'

'Would we?' a man asked. 'We use it for just about

everything on this trip. I'm George Wallace, Stella's husband. She had to go.'

Matt and Peter both half smiled, amused by the man's tone but feeling sympathy for the woman's discomfort.

'Suggest she drinks a weak solution of bicarb and water—she could mix sugar or juice into it to make it more palatable if she likes. It might help alkalise her urine and ease the burning sensation until the antibiotics begin taking effect. Where are you heading?'

'We thought we'd arrive at a very small dot on the map called Castleford by tomorrow evening,' the man explained. 'Should we try to hurry? Is there medical help there?'

'Unless Mrs Wallace gets worse you needn't hurry— in fact, it's best not to over those roads. There's a small hospital in Castleford run by a Sister Jensen. I'll let her know you're coming. She can test your wife's urine and hopefully confirm that it is cystitis and nothing more sinister. She knows our clinic pattern and if she thinks Mrs Wallace should see a doctor she'll either call us or direct you to the nearest clinic stop.'

'Bicarbonate of soda? Is that one of your old bush remedies?' Matt asked, when Peter had signed off and returned the handset to the top of the radio.

'What do you think's in the fizzy drinks we usually prescribe?' Peter asked. 'Good old bicarb with a bit of lemon flavouring in most of them. It hasn't been a universal panacea through the ages for nothing, you know!'

Matt grinned at him, liking this man he'd been so wary of at first meeting. And why had he been wary? he wondered. Then he remembered Lucia's reaction to

Peter—that slight withdrawal and the flush of colour beneath her fine, clear skin.

Lucia! Guilt and shame surged through him. He had to see her. Apologise for that presumptuous kiss! He glanced at his watch. After five! Would she have gone?

'Clock-watching already?' Peter asked with mock severity. 'Not good enough! Look at Katie over there— she should have left on the dot of five if she'd been a good union work-to-rules girl but, no, she hung in until I finished with the poor, uncomfortable Mrs Wallace before she signed over to the after-hours service.'

Katie spun around at the sound of her name and her clear hazel eyes flashed fire for a moment before she swung her curtain of hair to cover her face and turned away.

Matt watched the little byplay and wondered what it was between these two—but then remembered that Lucia would be getting further and further away from him. With more haste than neatness he packed the loose items back into the chest and returned it to the equipment room. Peter met him in the corridor.

'I'm on call so I'll hang around here for a while longer,' he said. 'There's always a bit of paperwork to catch up on.'

Matt smiled at him, secretly relieved that Peter hadn't suggested they do something together. It would have been hard to find an acceptable excuse after only a few days in town.

Saying goodbye, he walked quickly through the empty rooms, checking that Lucia wasn't still in the building. He had to see her but would calling at her house be intruding? During his visit to Australia he'd met many girls and all had been glad to introduce him

to their families and welcome him into their homes—
showing kindness to a visitor from a foreign land.

But Lucia? There was something different about her
and the only thing he did know for certain was that he
didn't want to start off on the wrong foot—if he hadn't
done so already with that impulsive, irresistible kiss.

Lucia had hurried home, trying to forget the feel of
Matt's lips on hers, but Aunt Steph's house wasn't the
sanctuary she needed because the memory refused to
stay outside. She showered and changed, dressing carefully, although he hadn't said he'd see her later—hadn't
made any arrangements at all! And he'd seen his patients
last night so there was no reason for him to go back up
to the hospital.

'There's a young man to see you, Lucia.' Her aunt's
voice echoed through the old house and hammered its
way into Lucia's heart. She spun away from the mirror,
frightened by the glowing eyes and flushed cheeks of
a girl she barely recognised.

Forcing herself to move sedately, she walked down
the long central passage towards the front door.

'But of course you must stay to dinner,' she heard
her aunt say, and felt the jolt of panic as her body
reacted faster than her mind.

'Dr Laurant tells me he would like to visit the hospital
with you tonight,' Aunt Steph told her as she reached
the veranda. 'I've insisted he eat with us.'

'Please call me Matt!'

His words to her aunt all but drowned out her shy,
'Hello,' and then they were swept along the veranda by
an imperious wave of her relative's arm and ushered
into the big kitchen that was the heart of the house.

'So, you are English and French. We are Australian and Italian,' Aunt Steph announced after an exhaustive interrogation of Lucia's new colleague, which had continued throughout the serving and consumption of a delicious meal.

Matt pushed away his plate.

'My family seem to make a habit of crossing the English Channel to marry. My French grandfather went to work in England as a young man, and met and married my grandmother there. Then my father did the opposite,' he explained. 'He went to France to study, met my mother, fell in love and stayed. He went home regularly to visit his family and I was educated in England, but my grandparents who lived in England are both dead now so my young sisters are completing their studies in France.

'My father says he is more French than English anyway, no matter what blood flows in his veins.'

Lucia smiled. The love that Matt felt for his family was evident in a special warmth in his voice and a softness in his eyes. She heard and saw and understood it because it was how she felt about her own family.

'And your own future?' Aunt Steph pursued. 'Do you think you might do the same? Meet a girl in this foreign country, marry here and settle down?'

Lucia's lungs stopped working. How could her aunt embarrass her like this? She looked across at Matt, dismay widening her eyes, but he couldn't have read anything other than interest into the question because he was shaking his head and smiling!

'Australia and France are a little further apart than England and France,' he pointed out. 'And I also have another stage of my career to consider.' He paused for a moment, and turned his head to include Lucia in the conversation.

'I did my medical degree in England where my father trained, and I have always planned to follow further in his footsteps and do my specialty training in France. We are building up our own tradition, you see.'

'Specialty training?' Lucia echoed, hoping to hide a shapeless ghost of fear that flitted across her heart.

He smiled again—the warm, sunny, confident smile of a man who has his future all planned out.

'I wish to specialise in ophthalmology—to be an eye specialist,' he explained. 'It is my father's field so I suppose, growing up with models of eyes for toys, it is not surprising. It was to study at a hospital in Paris that he travelled to France and met my mother.'

So, even if he falls in love with Australia he won't change his mind and stay, Lucia thought, recognising the dedication in his voice. Falls in love with Australia or with you? an inner voice jeered.

'So, Lucia, are you going to sit all night dreaming at the table or are you going to take Matt to the hospital and introduce him to your pet patients?'

She started and flushed, looking from her aunt to Matt, the heat strengthening in her cheeks as she saw him smile at her.

'We'll clear away the dishes first,' she said, pushing back her chair and trying to hide her confusion by looking busy.

'Go! Go!' her aunt insisted, waving them out of the kitchen with little shooing movements of her arms, exactly as if she was herding chickens out of her garden. 'And bring Matt back for a cup of coffee later. The

French part of him would probably appreciate my special coffee.'

If I get any hotter I will spontaneously combust, Lucia thought, muttering an incoherent excuse to Matt and fleeing to the safety of her bedroom. And why was Aunt Steph behaving this way—positively throwing her at Matt's head? The man had said that he had no intention of staying in Australia and her aunt must know that she, Lucia, could never leave.

He was sitting on the top step when she emerged, rising to his feet when he heard her sandals click across the old wooden floorboards. He reached out and took her hand, gave it a reassuring squeeze then held it, as if she might need his support to walk down the ten steps to level ground.

'I did not mean to intrude myself into your aunt's home—your home,' he said, dropping her hand and going ahead to open the gate and hold it for her.

As she passed in front of him she saw concern and a little embarrassment in his blue eyes, and her own confusion eased.

'No one says no to my aunt when she's in one of her organising moods,' Lucia assured him. 'Anyway. . .'

She had been going to say how pleasant it had been to have his company but as she spoke her gaze moved from his eyes to his lips, and she remembered the feel of them on hers—the texture and firmness and warmth—and the words vanished from her mind.

Her lungs tightened, trapping air, and tension twined about them, holding them enmeshed into a tableau of two people by a garden gate. Lucia felt the stillness, smelt the frangipani in the garden and the salt wind off the bay. She heard frogs rustle the grasses and flying foxes flap overhead—all senses on alert, poised and waiting, but for what?

His voice, when he finally spoke, was barely audible but deep and husky. Could he feel what she felt? Was he, too, frightened to break the spell that had woven them in its toils?

'I did not mean to kiss you in the equipment room yet now, when I should be apologising, I want to do it again.'

She didn't move, except to reach out a hand and grab hold of the gate so that she wouldn't fall down if the trembling in her legs continued to worsen.

He leant across it and once again his lips touched hers—cool at first, then warming with the fire that raced between them like an electric current. Lucia's fingers tightened on the palings, rough splinters digging painfully into her skin. But even the pain had an exquisite edge as she stood apart from this man she barely knew, touching only at the lips yet somehow joined to him within the very core of her being.

'Your patients will be wondering where you are.'

The words were murmured against her skin and she drew them into her mind and tried to make sense of them, but they became lost in the whirling chaos of her brain and she remained clinging to the gate like a sailor to a lifebelt.

Then he lifted his head, and she opened her eyes to see his profile etched against the violet velvet of the early evening sky. He slid an arm around her shoulders and drew her close, while his free hand reached out and unfastened her fingers from the paling.

'Would it be so bad for us to fall in love?' he asked,

guiding her out onto the footpath and turning in the direction of the hospital.

She turned to look at him, unable to believe that he could have divined her thoughts so accurately. And how was she supposed to reply? What did she know about love?

She couldn't remember her reaction to the few trial kisses she'd exchanged with Daniel but when Anthony had kissed her once or twice the ground had remained firm beneath her feet, her legs had stayed straight and supportive and her mind and body had continued to work to order.

'My parents fell in love when they were seventeen and they are still in love thirty-seven years later,' she said, although she had no idea where the words had come from and could see no relevance in them to this mad situation.

She heard him chuckle and felt the reverberations in the ribs that pressed against her side.

'So, to fall in love must lead to marriage and happy ever after. I thought as much, sweet Lucia,' he murmured, whispering the words so close to her ear she felt her hair moving with his breath. 'No falling in love for love's sake? Or because it is a nice thing to do?'

She knew he was teasing, but was there a doubt beneath the lightness in his voice?

Her feet kept moving, her body propelled by the arm around her shoulders, but her mind was barely aware of their motion. Back in some kind of working order, it was now absorbed by the new challenge this stranger's kiss had prompted.

'I don't know much about falling in love for love's

sake,' she told him, 'but it sounds a little like a fancy way of describing an affair.'

He gave a shout of laughter and hugged her closer to his side.

'I think it probably is,' he admitted, 'and somehow I don't think an affair is quite your style.'

They had reached the bottom of the hill that sloped up to the hospital, and he dropped his arm from around her shoulders and released her hand. She turned to face him, all the muddled thoughts now crystal clear in her mind.

'I've never had an affair,' she admitted, 'but I don't think it is, either.'

She spoke seriously. Let him think that she would only settle for marriage, she decided, knowing in her heart that it was not the reason for holding back. But to have an affair with him and then say goodbye at the end of the year would be one more loss in her life, and she couldn't cope with that. It would break a heart already bruised and battered by capricious fate!

He said nothing and, with the uneasiness within her churning faster in the silence, she found herself adding, 'I realise I've probably been more influenced by my parents and my upbringing than most girls are but an affair with a visiting doctor, no matter how well he kisses, wouldn't seem right.'

She had to force the words out, aware of how prudish and priggish they must sound.

His face seemed stern in the lamplight as he looked down into her eyes with a steady regard. Her heart thudded in her chest and she wished the stilted words unspoken, erased from the air and from his thoughts.

'And I am not a man to offer you an affair, Lucia,'

he said gravely. 'The very word implies an end before anything is begun. Whatever this attraction is between us, it deserves better than that.'

She tried to compute the words, to make some sense of them, but as she felt her brows drawing together in a puzzled frown he leaned forward and kissed the skin above her nose—like her mother used to kiss away the pain of a bruise or scratch.

'We'll sort it out,' he promised huskily, 'later!' Then his voice changed and he added with a bracing grin, 'When you've said goodbye to Lydia and read to Gilbert and you've introduced me to the brave and marvellous Carol who plans to return to her deep bush isolation and work the tin mine with her twin babies.'

She swung into step beside him, too fazed by all that was happening to do anything else. But the inner voice that had mocked her earlier now whispered caution. It would be very easy to be swept along by this man, especially as her heart and body seemed to enjoy the direction of his 'sweeping'.

But there could be no happy-ever-after in it, the voice reminded her, only more heartache and loneliness.

CHAPTER SIX

WITH an ease she found difficult to believe, Matt Laurant insinuated himself into her life until, two weeks later, Lucia found herself wondering if there had ever been a time when she hadn't woken thinking of him.

'Matt due back today?' her aunt asked at breakfast.

Trying to hide the heat that even hearing his name produced in her body, she nodded noncommittally and said, 'But don't go cooking a welcome home dinner. Clinic flights are notoriously late.'

It was the first two-day clinic he had done, and last night had been the first evening they hadn't seen each other since he began work at the base. And yet they'd done nothing special together—nothing that could even be called 'going out'. They walked to work together each morning, unless Matt had been on call and was either working or sleeping, and walked home together when their schedules fitted.

At the weekend she had taken him to the beach and shown him something of the town, walking through the familiar streets with a sense of rediscovery as they explored together.

But the evenings were their special time—the stroll to the hospital, and the lingering kisses in the deep-shadowed garden or on the veranda when they returned.

If Matt was working late Lucia would return alone to find him sitting on the steps, wanting to tell her about his day, to touch her hand, feel her skin and feast again on the softness of her welcoming lips.

'Going to take him home to meet the family?'

Aunt Steph's second question shook her out of her gentle reverie.

'There's no point, and you know it,' Lucia replied, more sharply than she'd intended. 'There's no future in it, Aunt Steph, so parading him at home will only upset Mum, who said she didn't want to see me back at the farm for at least six months, and probably annoy Anthony and his family—not to mention embarrassing Matt. We're friends, that's all,' she reminded her aunt, and left the kitchen before the drumming of her heart betrayed the lie.

He was sitting on the step when she returned from the hospital that evening, and, as she opened the gate she sensed a difference about him.

'And how was your trip?' she asked, giving her hand into the warmth of his and letting him tug her down onto the step beside him.

He didn't reply immediately, but drew her closer into his arms and buried his face in her hair as if the midnight blackness might hide him from whatever uneasiness he was feeling.

'I didn't like it much,' he admitted at last. She was tucked against his shoulder and she felt his chin, resting on the top of her head now, moving as he spoke. 'I'd been to Herd Island and Cabbage Tree, both aboriginal settlements, so I knew what to expect—but Caltura! I know why it's a full-day clinic.'

Lucia tried to remember what she knew of Caltura. There'd been a problem, she knew, but exactly what it was. . .

'Usually, in the settlements where there's no hospital there's an appointed health worker who knows which local people need to see us,' Matt continued. 'He or she collects the patients and brings them to the clinic so we go through the list in a fairly orderly way. There are all the usual things like flu and gastric attacks, sometimes teenagers with knuckle injuries from a fight that got out of hand; we check on tropical ulcers, eye problems, that kind of thing.'

His voice tailed away but Lucia had remembered what it was she'd heard.

'They had trouble keeping a health worker,' she said. 'I'm reasonably certain they didn't have anyone reliable on the ground out there for a long time.'

'Exactly!' Matt sighed. 'And now this fellow has turned up, and I'm not even certain that he's had any nursing or first-aid training. However, he's determined to get them organised but virtually has to start from scratch.'

Lucia wondered what he meant, but didn't ask. If he wanted to tell her he would and, in the meantime, it was nice to be sitting in his arms like this, bathed in the silvery light from the brilliant stars above and lapped by the scents and sounds of the garden's mysterious night-life.

'Do you know much of the ways of the aboriginal people?' he asked, and Lucia shook her head.

Matt sighed, and said, 'The people at Caltura have slipped so far behind the other places I've visited I can't help but wonder if they might have deliberately gone against whatever an unpopular health worker tried to tell them.

'Or they were upset because they had a number of

changes of doctor—first with James's predecessor, then James himself for such a short time, followed by the locum and, finally, me. That's at least four doctors they've seen in the last three months. And now, either because they've been offended in some way or because there's been no one to remind them about sensible health and hygiene practices, there are things happening that it is too late to control.'

'But we've still been doing regular clinic flights every fortnight!' Lucia protested.

'With a different doctor each time there's been a lack of observation and follow-up work! And what good is our visiting if there are no patients to be seen?' Matt asked. 'I checked through the records last night. Our people have seen the women who've come for pregnancy checks, immunised what kids have been attending school if they were due for shots and treated wounds, coughs and colds and injuries.'

'Isn't that enough?' Lucia asked, wondering about the concern she could feel in his tense body.

'No!' he said. 'This new chap out there, Andrew Walsh, has only been at Caltura a fortnight but he must have worked like a Trojan. He'd covered all the outlying areas and visited every family group. He persuaded people who hadn't been to a clinic for months to come back for check-ups, then picked them up and brought them in to make sure.'

'Which meant you were very overworked,' Lucia said, a little disappointed that this might be his complaint.

'I don't mind being overworked!' he erupted, pushing her away from him and turning her so that he could look into her eyes. 'I'd far rather be overworked, Lucia, than finish on time and worry I'd missed something.'

His hands bit into her shoulders and he gave her a little shake, as if the physical action might release some of his anger harmlessly.

'What upset me was the result of the neglect. To see things that could have been cured if treated earlier—to have to bring a man to town to have his foot amputated because no one was checking his foot care or insisting he follow his diet. The trachoma is so bad again that half the people I saw are almost blinded by it, and at least six will have to have surgery to repair their eyelids.'

'Will they have to be brought to town?' she asked, trying to envisage the magnitude of the problem he had faced.

His hands eased their grip on her shoulders, rubbing where they had seized earlier.

'No, I spoke to Jack last night. He'll arrange for a specialist to go next week. It seems they can arrange to drop him and a flight sister off, then pick the pair of them up next day. The way things are out there, I might go back again myself if Jack can shuffle the rosters. I've started all the trachoma cases on antibiotics and sulphonamide drops but, unless those people still unaffected stick rigidly to a hygiene routine of hand-washing and disinfecting towels and handkerchiefs, it will continue to spread.'

Lucia smiled at the determination in his voice.

'You see it as a personal challenge, don't you?' she teased, and saw his shoulders relax as he smiled back at her.

'On my soap-box, was I?' he asked, and ran his fingers through her hair, pushing it back from her brow as if he wanted to see her more clearly. 'I suppose it is a personal thing, because my interest has always been in eyes.' Now he ran his fingers through his own hair, searching for words that were eluding him.

'It's because it's such a preventable thing, trachoma,' he explained at last. 'And can be treated successfully. By rights, it should have been eradicated by now, but still it strikes at those who are most vulnerable and still it leads to blindness if we cannot treat it in time.'

Lucia nodded, feeling the empathy he had for the people he considered 'vulnerable' and loving him for it.

'And as well as that there are at least five patients whom I suspect have Hepatitis A and this could also spread like wildfire, a dozen or so with STDs, a collection of tropical ulcers and I wouldn't be surprised if as yet undiscovered parasites are infecting the intestines of another dozen. And that's not to mention kids with ear infections, fungal infections and impetigo. I've taken blood from just about everyone I saw, for one reason or another. There's a general debility among the people I haven't seen anywhere else.'

He sounded so depressed that Lucia wrapped her arms around him and drew him close to her body.

'You'll fix it,' she promised. 'I know you will. Especially if this new health worker stays.'

He pressed a kiss into the hollow at the base of her neck, sending tingling shivers up and down her spine, but his thoughts were not on kisses, she realised when he spoke again.

'Yes, Andrew!' he mused. 'He's quite a man, and something of a mystery, but it appears he has the welfare of the Caltura people at heart. He seems determined to make them take care of themselves.'

'Will they listen? Can he do it?' Lucia asked, her lips moving against the prickly stubble of his hair.

'He's big enough to make them do it,' Matt replied, moving so that her mouth slid across his temple, his cheek then met his lips—and conversation ceased.

The ramifications of Matt's concern were causing ripples through the calm waters of the base when Lucia arrived next morning. Matt had not met her on the way so she assumed that he'd been called out, but Jack had the look of a man who had been at his desk for many hours.

'Coffee might save my life,' he said to Lucia as she passed his door. 'And food,' he added. 'It's been a rough night.'

'There was an minibus accident on the Ruthven Road,' Christa told her while she made the coffee. 'A group of young backpackers in it. Swerved to avoid a roo, careered down a gully and hit a tree instead.'

'How were they found?' Lucia asked, knowing that it was one of the least used roads in their area.

'Pure luck!' Christa told her. 'Another group travelling in two four-wheel-drives had been delayed earlier in the day when one of their vehicles developed engine trouble. Rather than get behind in their schedule, they decided to push on through the night and caught a reflection of the back of the minibus in their headlights. They radioed base, and we sent two planes.'

'Two planes!' Lucia breathed the words. The extra plane seemed to multiply the horror in her mind.

'You OK?' Christa asked and Lucia managed to nod, forcing back the memories she still hated confronting

She busied herself with the coffee but as she placed

the tray carefully on Jack's desk her hands were trembling.

He looked up at her and she saw the understanding in his eyes.

'Doesn't ever seem to get any easier, does it, kid?' he said lightly but he reached out and clasped her hand, holding it until he felt the trembling cease.

'Of course, the best cure for these jitters of yours is work, and have I got some of that for you!'

He rolled his eyes skywards in such a ludicrous way that she had to laugh.

'It seems there've been problems at Caltura,' he said, his voice now deepening as his thoughts returned to his work. 'Problems I should have anticipated, damn it, and didn't.'

He looked up, and she saw the regret he felt mirrored in his eyes.

'Leonie has freed you for the day, so I'd like you to get all the Caltura files and go through them one by one. I'm not even certain what I'm looking for, Lucia, but I know they'll tell us something. Could you make a kind of graph that would show how often a person visited the clinic?'

'Using the computer—of course,' she assured him, pleased by the thought of a challenge. 'Should I show why they visited as well? I could do that using a box graph and then at a later date if you needed, say, the trachoma figures you could pull those out.'

'Oh, could I?' he asked, inclining his head towards her and smiling ruefully. She remembered that Jack was another doctor who put his trust in paper rather than bytes.

'Well, I could for you,' she relented. 'I'll get the files

and set it up. Will I use the radio room?'

It had big tables and more monitors than individual offices, so computer filing work was usually done in there.

'Sure,' he said absent-mindedly, his head already bent again and his mind on the mound of paperwork he accumulated so effortlessly. But, as she moved away, he looked up and smiled.

'I'm glad you came to work for us, Lucia,' he said, and added softly, 'Matt should be back about eleven.'

Heat shot into her cheeks. They had been so careful to appear as normal colleagues at work—which was all they were, really, apart from a few goodnight kisses!

'I saw you at the beach on Sunday, but haven't breathed a word here at the local gossip factory,' he added, answering the question in her eyes.

'He's just a colleague, a friend like all of you,' she spluttered. 'A stranger here and a neighbour. I've only been showing him a bit of the town.'

Jack's smile deepened but all he said was, 'He's a good man, Lucia,' and he bent his head again, silently dismissing her.

She stood in the passageway and took three deep breaths, her mother's remedy for panic, fear, nervousness and apprehension. They didn't work but the pause reminded her that she had a time-consuming but important job ahead of her, and she hurried away to get the files she needed.

A quick survey showed her that the easiest way to attack the job would be to update the computer files on all Caltura patients, then set up a programme to select the information she required and show it in different ways. The lure of discovery quickened her pulse, and she bent to the task with an eager willingness.

Matt had sounded so despairing when he spoke of what he had found at Caltura, yet he'd committed himself to setting it right. To be able to help him, even in this small way, was an added bonus—making the challenge something they could meet together.

'Both planes down, duty staff returning to base and on-call staff going home to sleep.'

She was so absorbed in what she was doing that she nearly missed the radio officer relaying the good news to someone. She looked up, saw Leonie in the room and smiled at her. At least she would understand the smile. What Jack knew Mrs Cooper also knew, but secrets were safe with the two of them.

The two of them? Now why would that make her stop and think? She smiled at the silly idea, shook her head and returned again to the disruptive pattern she was discovering in Caltura's medical service.

She heard the activity outside the radio room and knew that the flight staff were back. Matt will have gone straight home, she told herself, yet instinct told her he was here.

Susan came into the room first, her face grey with fatigue. Peter followed, stubbly-faced, his eyes reddened by tiredness and strain and then Matt, his face the least ravaged by the long night but waves of strain emanated from his body so strongly that Lucia had to curb the desire to reach out and hold him.

'Food and coffee, please, Lucia,' Jack said, and she knew he was sending her out of the room before the grisly details of the accident were revealed. She pushed the Caltura papers into a pile and left the room.

'I'll help.'

She heard Matt's words as she walked away and his footsteps, heavier than usual, following her. Inside the kitchen she waited and as he came through the door she pushed it closed behind him, moved into his outstretched arms and clasped her own around him, holding him in silence as if her warmth and energy might restore his resilience.

'I came because I had to see you for a moment—to hold you like this. I'm going home to have a sleep and then up to the hospital. The young tourists were all French- or German-speaking. I may be able to help with translation or contacting their families or simply talking to those who are well enough. I don't know what I can do but I feel I must go.'

'Of course you must,' Lucia agreed. 'But get some sleep first. Later, if you feel you can leave them, Aunt Steph would be glad to give you dinner.'

His arms tightened.

'I'll see you for dinner, then,' he murmured, releasing her as suddenly as he had reached for her. Lucia understood and crossed the kitchen, setting cups and sandwiches on a tray while he spooned coffee into the coffee-pot.

'It was bad—the accident?' she asked, and saw the regretful shake of his head.

'Two of the young men, if they survive Theatre, will go straight to Intensive Care. Both have head injuries and internal damage that was too difficult to assess at the site. Two of the girls, who were asleep at the time it happened, have escaped with almost minor injuries. One has a fractured collar bone and suspected breaks in her arm and wrist, while the other was concussed and cut about by broken glass.'

'They were the lucky ones?' Lucia prompted, filling the pot with boiling water.

'Very lucky,' Matt said. He picked up the tray and carried it out of the room. 'The other couple were in the middle of the minibus—one has spinal injuries, a suspected fracture in the lower thoracic or lumbar region and possible internal injuries, while the last one has a fractured femur, which is always a major trauma, and was heavily concussed.'

Lucia opened the door into the radio room and as she walked in behind Matt she realised they were discussing the person with the suspected spinal injuries.

'Do you want to stay and listen, Lucia?' Jack asked. 'It's entirely up to you but, as you'll be computerising the reports, you might like to sit in.'

He was watching her closely and she knew he was asking, Are you up to this? Are you ready to put the horrors of your own experience behind you?

Am I? she wondered, aware that she had to answer before people read anything into her hesitation.

'I—I'll stay,' she said, and slipped back into her chair at the second table. Matt was pouring coffee and the others had begun eating, replenishing energy reserves the night had drained from them.

'I wonder what's new in immobilising spinal patients before they are removed from the vehicle,' Peter said. 'I still believe that's where we can improve procedures and minimise further injuries.'

Susan explained what they had done and Lucia wondered if this was how they had removed her mother from the car, but then Jack was speaking again.

'There's a "First Hour" conference in the United States later in the year, Peter. I've been thinking some-

one from the Service should go. How about it? We
always try to keep abreast of new developments and to
ensure we have up-to-date equipment, but a conference
on trauma and pre-hospital care like that would give
you the very latest information and you'd have a chance
to see the gear they use in other places.'

Peter nodded, then Susan directed them on to the next
patient. As the session finished Matt stood up and left
the room, his lips tilting in a half-smile at Lucia as
he went.

She opened the Caltura files again as the others filed
out, but Jack paused at the table and touched her lightly
on the shoulder.

'OK?' he asked, too gently, and she looked up and
smiled at him through a sudden blurring of tears. But
her mother had been right! It was time to put away the
past. The silly tears were an acknowledgement of that.

'The individual patient numbers dropped off before
James began work,' she told him in a firm voice, determined to show him the new Lucia.

'But we'd have seen that straight away in the day
book,' he argued, taking his cue from her. 'I mean, it's
not hard to realise you've only filled in half a page of
appointments when normally you fill the page and go
over on to the next.'

'Not when it's masked by other factors. Look!'

She punched in a code on the computer and brought
up a copy of the day book page she wanted. Leonie
walked in and joined Jack, head bent towards the screen.

'This was the doctor before James—his last visit to
Caltura. See these names—' she highlighted over half
the names '—well, they're not Caltura people. They
were all new files that day and none of them had been

entered on the computer, although we have hard copies of their records.'

'So they were visitors,' Jack breathed, peering into the screen as if it might tell him something more. 'There was a dance festival at Caltura not so long ago. There could have been hundreds of visitors there, and you would expect more than a handful of patients from among those hundreds. But after that we should have noticed.'

Lucia tapped the keys again.

'This is the next week,' she said, displaying a much shorter list. 'It was James's first visit and you might expect shorter lists on first visits. By his next visit you're back to just over a page but, again, if I take these out—' she flicked a dozen names from the list '—you're down in numbers again. Those names I removed were all kids who'd been up to the coast for a Distance Education activity day and come back with mild food poisoning. The home tutor they use to help the kids with lessons would have insisted they see the doctor.'

Jack straightened and shook his head.

'I wonder if we've reached the stage where we need a computer clerk analysing the information all the time?'

He sounded tired and strained, and Lucia guessed that he blamed himself for the oversights that had led to the deteriorating health at Caltura.

'You can't blame yourself for staff changes,' Leonie reminded him. 'You try to keep the same doctor for each clinic flight if it's possible so that this kind of thing doesn't happen. At least that way the doctor knows who should be showing up for regular treatment and can send someone to fetch the laggards.'

'Yes, but we also rely a great deal on the health

worker. He or she must hunt up the regulars and make sure they come but, more than that, it is the person on the ground who sees that medication is taken and hygiene precautions are followed. They can't work miracles, I know, but most of them manage to remind patients about their tablets.'

'At daybreak and dark!' Leonie said with a smile and Lucia looked up at her, wondering what she meant.

'She's teasing me,' Jack explained. 'When I was still wet behind the ears I did a clinic flight to a settlement and, seeing smart watches and clocks around the place, assumed they had the same function they do in our culture.'

'He prescribed pills four-hourly, six-hourly or three times a day, according to what the book said, and flew happily off into the sunset.'

Lucia still looked puzzled, and Jack took up the explanation.

'It is a different culture to ours, and definitely not ruled by clocks. The clocks on walls showed affluence and watches were very acceptable jewellery, but there were only two definite times in most people's lives—daybreak and dark.'

He sighed then smiled.

'But even after I'd found substitute pills and potions that would work twice daily, there was still no guarantee they would remember to take them or apply them, or whatever.'

He flicked through the pile of files on the table.

'Could you get me a list of the people who used to see the clinic doctor every fortnight before this debacle began, and another list of those who saw him or her monthly?'

He turned to Leonie.

'Could we alter the rosters so Matt can go out there
again next Monday—one day only? I've got hold of an
eye specialist who's willing to go. And Katie,' he called
across to the radio officer who turned and smiled at
him, 'when Lucia has these lists I'd like you to get hold
of this new fellow, Andrew Walsh, at Caltura. I'll speak
to him.'

He patted Lucia's shoulder in a gesture that said
thanks and left the room with Leonie, discussing how
they could shuffle the roster to make the extra visit
possible.

She returned to the computer, feeding in the information it needed to produce the lists Jack wanted. For
some reason she felt more a part of the service than she
ever had before. Yet she had worked on filing medical
information often. Then an image of Matt's tired face
superimposed itself on the screen and she wondered if
it was because the work she was doing was connected
with him.

To work together! And to fly! The two things had
been her and Daniel's twin dreams from when they'd
first played together as children and watched the RFDS
planes passing overhead. He would be the doctor and
she'd be the nurse, he'd said—before she was old
enough to know what a nurse was. He'd learned about
the Service from an uncle who'd flown for it in the old
days, and told tales of landing on the main road into an
isolated town guided by the flare of kerosene-fed fires.

As names filled the screen in front of her she
recognised regret in her heart, but it was regret without
the pain she'd carried there too long. Daniel had been
part of her childhood, the boy next door who was first

best friend and later—tentatively and tenderly—a mild, exploratory first love. Close-lipped kisses beneath the mango tree, skinny limbs entwined—the way they'd hugged as children. Halfway to being grown-up, possibilities left in limbo.

'Are those the lists Jack's waiting for?' Katie asked as the printer chattered busily.

Lucia nodded, glad she'd pressed the PRINT command before she'd lost herself in the labyrinth of time past.

The phone rang and, as she crossed the room to tear off the lists for Jack, she heard Katie's voice.

'Did Matt go home?' she asked, putting the receiver carefully back into its cradle.

Lucia nodded, a new panic fluttering in her heart.

He needs to sleep, she wanted to cry out, but Katie didn't dial his pager number. Pulling a message pad towards her, she made a quick note.

'One of the patients is asking to see him, but later will do,' she explained. 'That was one of the high school teachers. She's up at the hospital translating for them at the moment, so it can't be urgent.'

Lucia smiled at Katie's pragmatic attitude. Like all the support staff at the base she obviously felt that her primary duty was to protect the medical staff, keeping them as worry-free as possible so that they could better perform the tasks they were employed to do.

Carrying the lists, she walked back to Jack's office but her mind was with the man sleeping not so very far away. Now that she'd finally said goodbye to Daniel, would she feel any differently towards Matt?

She shrugged.

There was no point, really, because nothing else had changed. Her mother was still an invalid, wheelchair-bound. She'd reluctantly accepted her mother's edict that she spend a year in town but Lucia still saw her mother's long-term care as her responsibility. She might be fourth-generation Australian but her Italian heritage was strong. She was the family's only daughter and she knew her duty.

She sighed, and admitted another point. It wasn't only duty—it was love!

CHAPTER SEVEN

As MATT walked up to the hospital later in the day he smiled as he passed Aunt Steph's house. How quickly he had become assimilated into life there. Lucia's hostess and relative had become his honorary aunt and he'd come to admire the common sense of her pronouncements, delivered in unusual, staccato bursts of words.

And how quickly he had grown to. . .

Like Lucia? Love Lucia?

Could it be love? he asked himself. Surely not!

Until today he'd thought it a fondness, but this morning he had needed to see her so badly that he'd returned to base instead of going straight home to bed. Then Jack had asked her if she wanted to sit in on the accident report. Asked her in a way that made Matt's heart hurt! Without knowing how, he had become aware that there were dark shadows in Lucia's past, holding her in a limbo of tantalising innocence—caught between adolescence and maturity at an age when most girls would consider themselves women.

He shook his head, clearing the fancies from his mind. Even if he was to fall in love with her, where would it lead? Lucia's feet were firmly fixed on Australian soil. Tales of his adventures left her breathless but there was no answering spark, no desire to emulate them or even go adventuring with him. And his life had been planned for so long that he did not want to think about deviating from his chosen path.

He lengthened his stride, hurrying away from his complicated thoughts.

The young woman behind the reception desk must have been watching for him. She beckoned to him as soon as he walked through the door.

'You're Dr Laurant?' she asked and, without waiting for an answer, added, 'Sister Cleeves asked me to send you up to Intensive Care as soon as you came in.'

His heartbeat quickened. Had one of the two badly injured tourists died? He thanked the woman and made for the lifts, sure of his way from his frequent visits with Lucia.

Although he had never been on this floor of the hospital the intensive care unit had more familiarity about it than other wards in the bright, airy building. The monitoring station, with its banks of screens and dials, was similar to all the others he had seen and the individual rooms, glass-walled to make visual observation possible, looked much the same. Even the intent hunch of the male charge nurse watching the screens reminded him of other times and other places.

Until he obeyed a signal from the nurse in one of the rooms and stepped inside!

It was like an oasis of calm. All the usual monitors were in place but the familiar wheezing and beeping of the machinery was so low that it was almost inaudible. The young man who had been driving the minibus lay as still as death itself, while machines pumped air into his lungs, worked his heart, dripped liquid and drugs into his veins and probed the secret workings of his brain.

The nurse straightened up from an inspection of the patient's urinary output, shaking her head. Without a word she adjusted a small covering over the young man's private parts, then led Matt out of the room.

'There's no urine output,' she explained. 'Dr Warren ordered a rapid infusion of fluids, then 10 mg Lasix intravenously, but there's been no response. He's coming back any minute but the monitors...'

She took him around behind the bank of screens but it was only when she introduced him to the charge nurse that he realised how she knew him. She was one of the nurses he'd met when he'd lunched with Peter—a lively redhead who had flirted harmlessly with him over a prawn salad.

There was no time for social nicety. The monitors showed that the young man was losing his battle and, as Matt watched, the line on the EEG screen levelled out and alarm bells sounded.

'The young girl with the spinal injury is in Ward Four A,' the nurse said quickly to Matt. 'She's heavily sedated but has been extremely restless. This fellow's her boyfriend. Could you go and see her—maybe sit with her a while?'

She paused and watched as the doctor rushed in and followed the charge nurse into the young man's room.

'I've got to take over the monitors,' she added, turning away from Matt to concentrate on the screens of two other patients in the unit. 'Just tell her you've seen him, nothing more,' she warned as he walked away.

Janet Cleeves! He remembered her name too late to say goodbye properly. And he didn't even know the young man's name.

He made his way to Four A, where the girl with long blonde hair and unseeing eyes the colour of cornflowers lay, her fingers plucking ceaselessly at the sheet that covered her.

'I can't see him,' she was muttering and Matt was surprised that, although she said the words in German, his mind translated them into English, not French. He grasped the restless fingers and sat down beside the bed, running his thumb back and forth across her hand in a soothing motion.

'I've seen him for you,' he said quietly, hoping that his German would be understood. 'They are taking such good care of him.'

His heart felt heavy at the lie but he knew that she was only semi-conscious and unlikely to remember anything he said. The important thing was to relieve her mind so that she could sink into proper, health-promoting sleep.

'It's very peaceful up there,' he continued, thinking back to his surprise when he entered the room. 'Usually, critical care units are noisy, unrestful places but these people seem to have got it right. The light's not too bright and the machines must have silencers on them they're so quiet.'

The fingers ceased their agitation and lay limply in his but he kept talking, concentrating on technicalities so that he didn't subconsciously reveal any emotion.

'In many units like that it's almost impossible to sleep for longer than ten minutes because of the noise, fifteen-minute assessments by the nursing staff and bright, glaring lights, but this place is different.'

He sensed that she was sleeping, but when he tried to withdraw his hand the fingers tightened on his.

'I worked in a hospital in Hamburg once,' he told her. 'Now there's a beautiful city.'

He was still remembering Hamburg when a nurse stopped by the other side of the bed.

'Are you a friend?' she asked, obviously disconcerted to find him there. She reached for the girl's wrist and took her pulse while she waited for Matt's reply.

'I'm a doctor,' he explained, 'but I'm not here as a doctor. I speak French and German and I thought I might be some help.'

'You've certainly helped here,' the woman replied. 'She's been so agitated we were considering increasing her sedation but Doctor didn't want to do that when she's been concussed.' She was efficiently pumping a blood pressure cuff, her observations not hampered in the least by her conversation.

'You're the new Flying Doctor, are you? I'd heard they had a Frenchman for a change.'

'For a change?' Matt repeated, and the woman looked up from writing on the chart to reply.

'Well, they get a lot of English and Irish doctors but I haven't heard of a French one before.' She sounded slightly doubtful, as if the credentials of a French doctor might be suspect.

'I did my training in England,' he said, 'but for family reasons, not because the French training system isn't excellent. The problem is the waiting time for foreign doctors to gain their accreditation in Australia. That might be why fewer European doctors join the Service. The arrangements for accreditation between the United Kingdom and Australia have been in place a long time, and doctors go back and forth between the countries frequently.'

The woman nodded, apparently satisfied with his explanation.

'The other two girls you brought in from the same

accident are in this ward,' she told him. 'Will you see them while you're here?'

Matt glanced at his watch. Aunt Steph usually had dinner on the table at six-thirty—a habit she'd acquired to accommodate Lucia's evening hospital visits.

Lucia! He couldn't think about Lucia now!

'Yes, I've time for a quick visit,' he said, 'then I'll come back later in official visiting hours.'

The slight, dark girl he'd lifted from the wreck was asleep, one arm encased in plaster from above the elbow to the wrist. The injured limb was strapped to her body at the moment and he remembered that they'd suspected a fractured clavicle, as well as injuries to the forearm and wrist. The strapping would prevent the arm moving while she slept. No doubt it would be replaced by a sling when she was more alert.

The third young woman was in the next bed and Matt sensed her watching him. He turned, dismayed by the criss-cross of stitches he could see beneath the light gauze dressing on her face.

'I'm Matt Laurant,' he said, introducing himself in polite German and offering his hand to her. 'How are you feeling?'

Tears welled in light, browny-golden eyes, and a puffiness of the lids told him she'd been crying for some time. She was the least injured so probably the most aware of what had happened to her friends, he thought sympathetically.

'Look at me!' she cried, her German less fluent than he would have supposed. 'Look at my face!'

He ignored the self-pity in the comment and asked, 'Are you French? I heard you were a mixed group but didn't know who was who.'

'I'm Swiss,' she snapped, startling him with the force-fulness of the assertion. 'But look at me! Look what they have done to me here in this dreadful place.' She was speaking French now, but the words were spat out with a viciousness that surprised Matt.

'They had no right to treat me!' she asserted. 'I should have been flown straight home. My father, my insurance—someone would have paid. I should have had experts, plastic surgeons—not butchers at some bush hospital down here.'

Matt drew a deep breath, momentarily glad that the woman wasn't French, but every country had its share of difficult people, he reminded himself. The thought failed to calm him and anger burned through him like an ulcer pain—flaring, searing into his stomach.

When he had examined this young woman, swaddled in blankets beside the vehicle, he had thanked God that one of them had been saved from permanent or disabling injury. Although the others had needed more urgent attention, Peter, while he worked to restore fluid to the driver, had instructed Allysha, who had left the plane to help wherever she could, in placing moist dressings over the girl's face to conserve the integrity of the damaged skin as much as possible.

Peter had given thought to the repairs a surgeon would have to do and to the effect that any facial scarring might have on a young woman's life, and taken pains to minimise it. And here she was, complaining loud and long about the treatment she'd received.

'The surgeons here are as skilled as any I have seen anywhere,' he said firmly, not adding that he was hardly an expert in reconstructive or microsurgery. 'Your face might look bad now and it will look worse when the

bruising comes out and you turn yellow and purple—'
he felt a quite unmedical delight in mentioning this to
the spoilt madam '—but there will be little scarring in
the end. The wounds were mostly superficial.'

'How would you know that?' she demanded. 'I nearly
bled to death in that accident. And the people that came
didn't seem to care at all.'

'Did you speak to them?' he asked, surprised by the
statement. She'd been unconscious when they'd arrived
at the scene, moaning and writhing in her makeshift bed.

'Of course! I told them to help me out.'

She must have been able to move her legs, Matt
realised. The travellers who'd found the wreck had
decided that there was no danger from fire and, remembering instructions about not shifting accident victims
in case they had spinal injuries, had left the other five
victims strapped in their seats. They had concentrated
on stemming bleeding and keeping them warm until
medical help had arrived.

His thoughts returned to this patient. Concussion, then
sudden clarity of mind followed by further, deeper
unconsciousness? It was a classic presentation of epidu-
ral haematoma, he thought, then realised that she was
very much awake and lucid now. He would have liked
to look at her chart but felt he was better playing the
innocent hospital visitor at the moment.

'I'll be coming up again later,' he told the girl, who
still hadn't introduced herself. 'Is there anything I can
bring you? A magazine, perhaps?'

'A mobile phone,' the girl said. 'I had one with me but
who knows where my belongings are now? I'll report it
to the police if anything's missing. I've heard of people
looting at the scene of accidents,' she muttered, 'and I

know out there it could only have been those people
who came along or the ambulance people or whoever
they were who brought us here.'

He ignored the inference to dishonest Service staff
with difficulty.

'I'll see if I can find out what happened to your
things,' he told her and hurried away, wondering how
her fellow-travellers had coped with such a selfish ego-
tist in their party. But perhaps her behaviour was a result
of shock. Then he realised that she hadn't enquired
about her fellow-travellers and his distaste for her
behaviour grew.

He glanced at the dark-haired girl as he passed her
bed and prayed that she would have a kinder nature.
The lovely blonde was going to need a lot of support
when she was told that her boyfriend had died.

At the nurses' station he asked if anyone had considered haematoma, explaining that she'd been
conscious at some stage at the accident site.

'We're watching all of them for any altered state in
their consciousness,' the nurse assured him. 'That one's
been conscious since she came in to us.' Matt imagined
he heard a silent 'unfortunately' uttered into the air.
'She speaks quite good English and, although she's
complained about the stitches, facial pain, lack of luggage and the nursing service, she hasn't complained of
a headache.'

She went on to tell him that the police had all the
luggage the RFDS personnel had brought back from the
site. The three women and one of the men had been
identified from passport photos, but two of the photos
were too similar to make positive identification possible.
Sadly, these two were the men who had been in the

front seat and were now in Intensive Care.

Matt wondered about the sixth passenger, the man with the femur fracture. If he'd had an open reduction, he would probably still be sleeping. The unhappy young woman with the stitched face was the only member of the party who would be rational enough—if such an adjective could be applied to her—to help the police with their problem.

'Good luck to them,' he murmured and hurried away, wanting to forget the problems of other people for a little while and enjoy his time with Lucia.

She heard him coming up the steps and hurried to intercept him, anxious to see if he looked rested—less strained.

They met on the veranda and he reached out and took her in his arms. Heedless of her aunt or any consequences, Lucia responded as her heart dictated, moving closer and holding him tightly. She lifted her head and their lips met, warm with the promise of sharing and caring—of affection and friendship. Of love?

'Did you sleep? Have you been to the hospital? I rang earlier for follow-up and was told one of the two patients in Intensive Care was not expected to live.' Lucia broke away first, pushing her body a little clear of his but maintaining contact with her hands on his hips.

She was trying to be objective about all this but her feelings towards Matt—this unfamiliar and unexpected attraction—had stirred her emotions into a soupy mess. Shreds of the past bubbled away with her fears of the future, while the sheer bliss of the present was clouded by the accident and the tenuous hold two of the victims had on life.

He drew her close again, and she wondered if her voice had betrayed her turmoil.

'If we have helped save five of them that's five families who won't suffer the ultimate anguish and heartbreak,' he soothed her. His blue gaze scanned her face and she tried to smile and pretend she was all right, but he wasn't fooled by the tremulous effort. With purposeful movements, he pushed her hair back from her face and ran the tip of his index finger down the long, fine scar that ran from two inches above her left temple to her ear.

'Was it a car accident?' he asked, and she nodded.

'Will you tell me about it?'

She looked at him and knew that, perhaps one day, she could.

'Not now,' she said. 'We've got to eat. You might have done your hospital visiting for the day but I still have to go up there and see my regulars.'

She spoke lightly but watched his face intently. Was he tired of spending all his days at work and his evenings visiting a hospital? She knew it wasn't a normal off-duty occupation for young people, although it had suited her and made her feel more settled when she'd first arrived at the Bay.

'I'm going back with you,' he told her, the words warming her blood nearly as much as his kisses had. 'I want to see them all again.'

He didn't say why but something in his voice made Lucia wonder if things were worse than she had thought. She held his hand as they walked around towards the kitchen, offering support she could not put into words.

'You on duty or on call this weekend?' Aunt Steph asked Matt as they sat down at the table.

'On call,' he replied. 'Why?'

'I've two tickets for a play at the amphitheatre,' she told him in her usual abrupt manner. 'Saturday night. You can be on call there as easily as anywhere else. Why don't you and Lucia go? They can page you if they need you.'

Before Lucia could regain enough breath to protest about this organising of her life Matt had asked, 'Amphitheatre?'

'Far end of the beach. It was a quarry and an eyesore before the council finally decided they'd better do something about it. Made it into an open-air theatre. Best in winter, of course, when there's less rain but a bit of cyclonic wind and wetness can add marvellously realistic effects to *Macbeth* or *The Tempest*.

'Aunt Steph did the landscaping of that whole foreshore area,' Lucia explained, although she was still apprehensive about her aunt's unsubtle suggestion.

'It sounds a great idea. I'd love to go,' Matt said, turning to smile at Lucia and obviously expecting her to share his delight.

She nodded, and let a smile tease her lips apart. It would be fun to go somewhere different with Matt. He had turned away to ask her aunt more about the landscaping project and she watched his alert expression as he listened, seeming to absorb the information through all his senses. His skin was smooth, a shade darker than when he had arrived but a golden brown that made his eyebrows and short, short hair seem fairer, glinting with golden highlights.

She remembered his cheek rubbing against hers earlier today, scratchy with stubble, and then again this evening, smooth and soft. Would all his skin have that same satiny texture? she wondered, then shivered as her nerves tweaked the most sensitive parts of her body to life, making her aware of it in a way she had never been before.

She knew that she wanted to feel that skin—to touch it and taste it and smell it—but her imaginings made her feel ashamed of herself and she tried to push them away from her mind. She glanced at Matt and the images recurred. Did he feel the same way about her?

'We'd better go.'

She blinked at the words, startled that she could have been so oblivious to her surroundings and the conversation at the table that she had almost jumped at the sound of his voice.

As they walked home he told her about the young man who had died and the despair of the girl who had loved him.

Now was the time to tell him about the accident; to tell him about Daniel, and dreams, and her mother, and Anthony. She thought about how she'd start but the words wouldn't come so, instead, she held his hand more tightly and when they reached the shadowy veranda she responded to his kisses with a desperation that fanned the smouldering desire between them into roaring, near-engulfing flames.

It began quietly enough with their arms around each other, nuzzling and teasing at ears and eyes and chin and lips—a sensual exploration of features, a teasing enticement to more as warm, breathy kisses lingered on the pleasure sensors in heated skin.

But when he kissed her, long and deep, her lips parted, accepting the probing of his tongue with a hunger she had never felt before. She pressed her body harder into his, her hands fierce in their possession of his back, his neck, his head, holding him to her as if only he could carry her into this next phase of her life.

Something changed between them and all conscious thought ceased. The slow-burning fuse of desire which had been running through her body since Matt first kissed her hit the well of emotional dynamite that had lain dormant for too long.

She felt her breasts go taut with a strange kind of pain and a tiny moan escaped her captive lips as she moved the tingling heaviness against his chest, seeking release from this new torment.

Somehow, without parting, they crossed the veranda so that she was leaning against the wall, glad of the support for a body in revolt. Matt murmured soft words against her mouth while one hand pushed at her hair tugging and teasing through it, and then the same fingers were on her neck, trailing fire along her nerves.

Did he know her pain? He pressed the wandering hand against one breast, easing for a moment the heavy ache, then his fingers skimmed across her skin above the low-cut neck of her light cotton top, sending new waves of frenzy along her overwrought nerves.

'Please, Matt,' she whispered against the ceaselessly insistent lips, but she didn't know what she was asking.

'I know, Lucia,' he murmured back, then dipped a finger deep between her breasts, releasing shudders of desire through her body. Her hands slid lower down his back, pulling his hips towards her. The hardness was a shock but when it brushed against the sensitised mound between her thighs she nearly cried with the unexpected pleasure.

His kisses gentled but she wanted more, moving the

lower part of her body against his and gripping him as
if she depended on his strength to stay upright.

She felt him sigh against her mouth and the response
as his kisses deepened once more, his fingers returning
to the tantalising exploration of her breasts. Now one
slid inside her bra and she flinched from the unexpected
delight, turning her head away from his kisses so that
she could concentrate on the new sensation.

Her mouth brushed against the roughness of his short
hair and she nipped at its stubbly feel with her teeth,
while his lips explored her neck and his thumb brushed
her nipple. Again she hid the groan of delight that threatened to erupt, biting her lip to capture the sound before
it could escape. Her body had taken on a life of its own,
responding not to her commands but to the magic of
Matt's hands, and lips and tongue.

Matt groaned, the sound warm on her skin, and
straightened up, still holding her so that his heat was
hers. He peered into her face in the dim light.

'You're not a girl for an affair,' he reminded her,
grinding out the words he'd said once before. 'I know
that, Lucia,' he added, shaking his head as if ashamed
of his own stupidity, 'and I didn't want things to get
out of hand.'

'And this is out of hand?' she asked shyly, half smiling at the self-condemnation in his voice.

'This is very out of hand,' he said, brushing his body
lightly against hers so that she felt the straining hardness
of his arousal. He lifted one hand and ran his fingers
down her cheek. 'And so is your response, my love,'
he told her gently, dropping his hand so that it brushed
against her breast on its way to settle at her waist.

'Why shouldn't we have an affair?' she argued, for-

getting all her own convictions in her disappointment—
feeling like a child who's been denied a treat. 'Most
girls my age have had dozens of affairs!'

He smiled at that and she felt a surging rush of love
for this man she'd known such a short time.

'Because you're not most girls,' he told her, dropping
the lightest of light kisses onto her lips.

'But I wouldn't mind, Matt,' she heard herself say,
while part of her mind reeled in horror. She was practically begging him to ravish her, she realised, all thoughts
of proper behaviour—all memories of Anthony's place
in her life—blown away by the temptations of delight
his body had offered her.

He studied her face for a moment and shook his head.

'We feel like this about each other because we are
falling a little in love and our bodies are already attracted
to each other,' he explained. 'If we take it the next step
further—to a physical relationship—two things could
happen.'

He sounded very serious and she tried to concentrate,
but the waves of awareness were still short-circuiting
her nerves and the messages to and from her brain were
as scrambled as Aunt Steph's breakfast eggs.

'We might find that it's a purely physical thing and,
when our bodies have enjoyed themselves for a few
months, the urgency and heat will die away and we will
part good friends.'

Lucia weighed the words as carefully as her bemused
brain would allow and decided that he didn't sound very
convinced about this. It didn't sound very convincing
to her either but, then, she had no experience against
which she could judge.

'Or?' she prompted, sliding one leg up and down so

that one of her thighs could rub against his while they talked. His legs felt so hard against hers—a muscled bulk that fascinated her with its solidity.

He moved a little restlessly but not away from her slow movement, she realised, then his arms tightened around her body.

'Or we might find whatever we feel for each other deepens and develops!'

The words came hesitantly from his lips as if his command of English had suddenly dried up. He smiled and shook his head, then continued, 'I'm sorry, Lucia, but I don't know the answer. I only know I've never felt like this before—not at any stage of an affair, and I haven't had that many—or with any other woman. Usually I know that it will be an enjoyable interlude for both of us but that is all it will be. With you, I feel I might want more and it frightens me, my love.'

He paused and it was her turn to raise her fingers to his face and trace the features that were becoming so familiar to her.

'It terrifies me!' she whispered, feeling the pain of loss in her heart already although his year at the Bay had barely begun.

'Unless. . .' he said, and in the darkness she felt his lips tremble on the word and wondered what he hadn't said.

You don't want to know, some scrap of sanity warned, but she ignored it and echoed the word.

'Unless?'

He drew away from her now and led her out of the shadows into the muted light that shone through the glass-panelled front door. Here he looked into her face,

waiting for reaction, but in his eyes she saw defeat, as
if he had already anticipated it.

'Unless you feel you'd be prepared to come back to
France with me,' he said, the words tumbling over each
other in their rush to be said. 'I wouldn't want that
commitment now, Lucia, but I would like to know it
might be possible. I'd like to think if what we have is
really love it would not have to end when my year here
is finished and I return home.'

Lucia felt the words dancing in her brain, frothing
on the cloudy soup. It's a kind of proposal, she realised.
A promise to commit myself to him if things work out
that way.

A promise I cannot make!

The thought washed over her like a tumbling wave,
leaving her so cold that she seemed to feel splinters of
ice in her veins.

I can't say no without explaining.

The second thought was no better, she decided, and
it did little to warm her frozen feelings. She took a deep
breath, then tried another one for luck.

I don't need three, she said in a silent message to her
mother.

'Would you like a cup of coffee?' she asked.

CHAPTER EIGHT

'So, YOU have a mother, a father and four brothers all much older than you who have married and moved away from home,' Matt summed up as Lucia slid a cup of frothy cappuccino in front of him and dropped into a chair at the end of the table.

'But my mother's in a wheelchair!' She blurted out the words, uncertain how she was going to approach the rest of the story.

'Ah!' he said softly, reaching out to cover her hands with one of his. 'As a result of an accident.'

It could have been a question but it wasn't and she looked at him, puzzled by his assumption. There were so many medical reasons why people might become wheelchair-bound.

'Jack was very gentle with you today,' he explained, his voice husky with sympathy, 'when he asked if you wanted to sit in on the accident discussion.'

Lucia nodded.

'Jack and Mrs Cooper know about it,' she admitted. She drew one hand out from the protective covering of his and busied herself drawing invisible patterns on the polished table-top.

'I was six years younger than my closest brother so, in many ways, I was like an only child,' she said, her eyes on the patterns she couldn't see. 'When I was four a new family came to work on the farm.'

She paused, looking up at Matt, and saw the eyes she

loved to watch filled with concern—for her.

'Did I tell you my father farms sugar cane?'

He nodded and she continued, her head erect now, watching his face for his reactions.

'The new people had a son called Daniel who was my age—we even shared a birthday. We became playmates, then friends, then. . .'

Her gaze met Matt's and clung there, silently willing him to understand. Her throat was thick with unshed tears and old emotional scars tearing loose.

'As we grew up he was my first love,' she whispered. 'We shared our first kiss, the first embraces of adolescence. We always knew, right from the beginning, that we would stay friends for ever, and then later we thought we'd be lovers and marry—one day, some time—'

She blinked away the dampness in her eyes, and half smiled at Matt.

'Daniel was quick and clever and imaginative, as natural a leader as I was a follower. He made up our games; he organised our holiday time together and he planned our future.'

'In the Flying Doctor Service?' Matt murmured, and Lucia blinked in surprise. Had she told him that?

'Yes,' she said, smiling more broadly now at the memories she'd hidden away too long. 'He was crazy about the Service. Talked about it all the time. He was going to be the doctor and I would be the nurse, and we would run one of the smaller bases and save lives every day.'

'So?' Matt prompted gently, and Lucia drew the third breath.

'We were fifteen when his parents decided he should go to boarding-school for his final two school years to

make certain he would qualify to study medicine. We
both kicked up such a fuss that it was agreed I would
go, too. We were so excited, Matt,' she said, looking
into his eyes again as she tried to convey the occasion.
'It was to be the best adventure we'd ever had—the
first time I would ever go in a plane. We were to fly
south from Rainbow Bay and Daniel's father was to
drive us to town—the two of us and my mother.'

Matt felt his skin grow cold, guessing what was to
come. His hand tightened on Lucia's fingers as if he
could already feel her slipping away from him. He knew
the competition now—not only a mother in a wheelchair
but a beloved ghost as well!

'I can't remember anything about the accident,' she
was saying when he pulled himself together enough to
listen. 'I can only tell you what I was told.'

With limping, halting words and phrases she eased
out the story, while Matt's vivid imagination and recent
experience coloured it with pain and shock and horror
and blood.

'Because the car was halfway down the slope and
one false move could have plunged it to the bottom,'
Lucia explained, 'it took a long time to get us all out.
I know my mother went first and then Daniel's father,
who later had to have the lower part of his left leg
amputated. But Daniel and I were in the back and we
had to wait until they cut the car open before they could
lift us out. We were holding hands but they said he'd
been dead since it happened.'

Matt felt her pain, yet knew from her composure that
it was time she told the story. His free hand brushed
moisture from her cheek, his fingers moving on to linger
in her hair where the long scar was hidden.

'I was in a coma for a long time,' she told him. 'Then in hospital for several months after I came out of it. I. . .'

Her eyes beseeched his understanding and he frowned, not knowing what it was she wanted from him. The hand that lay quiescent beneath his on the table was cold, yet slick with sweat, and he knew what an effort this conversation was proving for her.

'I had to learn to walk again,' she whispered, and he felt his reaction surge through him. Traumatic shock! He'd heard about cases where there were no physical reasons for paraplegia.

He looked at the forgotten coffee, cold and flat on the table in front of him, and stood up, stepping across to Lucia's chair and bending to lift her in his arms.

He half turned and sat down again, holding her on his knee so that he could rub warmth back into her arms and use his hands and lips and body to say the words he knew would be inadequate.

'But you did learn to walk again, my love,' he muttered, desperate to bring her out of the past. 'Tell me about your mother. Did she injure her spine?'

He felt her nod against his neck, and tightened his hold on her body.

'We were both in hospital here at the Bay and one day, when they wheeled me in to see her, she'd just been told she would never walk again.'

The words were like a warm breeze on his skin and he sat very still, not wanting to halt the flow again.

'I remember her telling the doctor if that was the case she'd have to stay in hospital for ever because her husband and sons had a farm to run. They didn't have time to be fussing over an invalid.'

He felt her draw air deep into her lungs and waited.

She stirred and pushed herself away from him so that he could see her face. Her brown eyes were tear-washed and tiny droplets caught the light like diamonds in her thick, matted lashes.

'Hearing my mother say that to her doctor gave me the incentive to walk again, if nothing else,' she told him, one corner of her sweetly curving mouth curling into a semblance of a smile. He smiled back, although his throat was clogged with emotion, and her smile broadened.

'I've wondered since if she said it deliberately,' she admitted, the love she felt for her mother shining from her eyes. 'As soon as I could walk and she was stable we went back home, and caring for her kept me going until I could face people. She nagged at me until I found the courage to go back to school, two years behind my old classmates but there, where Daniel and I had been together.

'When I finished school she wanted me to go away to study, but when she didn't argue too hard I knew her urging was part of her unselfishness. I had no desire to go, anyway. No ambition or need to spread my wings or thirst for adventure. So I stayed, happy to be at home, until she tossed me out this year—like a bird throwing its fledgling out of the nest, she said—insisting I move to town and ''live a little''.'

'So you can go back to looking after her after you've sown your wild oats,' Matt teased, pressing little kisses against her temple.

Lucia stiffened in his arms and he knew he'd said the wrong thing.

'She would never expect me to give up anything in my life for her,' she told him vehemently. 'Looking

after her when we both left hospital gave me a reason
to keep living. Seeing how stoically she suffered and
how courageously she fought to regain whatever independence she could has made me what I am, Matt.'

• 'A brave, courageous, beautiful young woman,'
he said.

'A young woman to whom her family is doubly precious,' she pointed out. 'However much I enjoy living
in town and working at the base—and knowing you,'
she added with a rosy blush, 'my family are my life
and I know I will always want to be near them. I want
to go back to looking after my mother after this time
in town, not necessarily living with her but close enough
to help her with her personal tasks.

'Not because of duty or because she would expect it,
but because I want to be able to do that for the rest of
her life, Matt. Can you understand that?'

'Yes, Lucia,' he murmured, his heart heavy with all
the new love he felt for her. 'I can understand that.'

They sat in silence, arms wrapped around each other.
Matt absorbed her words into his heart as well as his
mind, and did understand. He wanted this girl-woman
as he'd never wanted anyone, yet something warned
him to stop the relationship right now. Taking that next
step into intimacy could lead him to pleasure and love
beyond anything he had experienced before. And if that
happened would he be able to walk away at the end of
one short year?

She stirred and he became conscious of her weight
on his knees and then conscious of her body in a
different way.

'Time for bed,' he whispered into the dark curls.
'We'll talk again tomorrow.'

'And the next day, and the next?' she asked uncertainly.

It was his turn to smile and shake his head with a rueful sadness.

'As friends, if nothing else,' he promised. 'I couldn't not be friends with you now—although I don't know how hard that will prove to be.'

He kissed her lips but the leaping hunger of her earlier response was gone, swept away by other tensions.

'I'm off duty tomorrow and will go up to the hospital in the morning to see what I can do for those young people. Why don't I call for you at six and take you up to the Pier for dinner? I've heard it has the best seafood in town.'

Lucia eased herself away from the warmth of his body. He was asking her out! Was he embarking on a pre-affair courtship after all? She thought about it and found small pockets of excitement in her mind.

'That would be very nice,' she said primly, but her body was stirring back to life and she remembered the dangerous exhilaration she'd felt earlier and understood what people meant when they talked about playing with fire.

His goodnight kiss was as restrained as her words but the hands that lingered on her shoulders, held by a magnetism he seemed unable to control, told her that the restraint was a supreme effort of will and the pockets of excitement filled and overflowed, spilling along her bloodstream and sparking her nerves to new life.

'We'll talk tomorrow,' he repeated. She felt her own hands move, as if pulled by invisible strings, to draw him close against her body. She forced them back to her side and clenched her hands into fists to stop them touching him.

Matt walked away, his mind repeating Lucia's story until the insistent summons of the pager drew his thoughts back to work. He jogged towards the base, remembering a similar journey in the early hours of the morning. The twenty-four hour 'on-call' shifts went from 6 p.m. to 6 p.m. He was officially off duty.

But so had Peter been last night, he reminded himself. Was this another two-plane emergency or had Jack already been called out?

The bright lights at the base welcomed him, and he was pleased to find Christa already waiting for him. He had worked with her at Caltura and enjoyed her quiet competence.

'It's Mrs James on "Seven Hills" station,' she told Matt. 'We took her home three weeks ago after her second lot of chemotherapy. She has breast cancer but had been in remission for eighteen months following a mastectomy and treatment. Came down for a regular check three months ago and a scan showed metastases in the brain and liver. She was in hospital here for nine weeks until the doctors considered she was well enough to return home.'

Christa was bent over the second drawer of filing cabinet while she explained this, and Matt watched her leaf through the folders.

'Her file is in the radio room. They don't have phone contact so Katie came in when the radio signal was picked up by the answering service,' she added. 'I'm looking for a paper Jack wrote on treating patients who could be approaching an immunosuppressed or thrombocytopenic state.'

She straightened and waved a slim folder in the air.

'OK,' she said, 'let's go. Eddie Stone's flying us and you're going because Jack is, at this very moment, on the operating table himself. Appendix, of all things!'

Matt shook his head in amazement as he followed Christa out the door. Were all Australians as 'laid back' as the people who worked at the base? They seemed to accept the most bizarre occurrences with a casual shrug and a calm, 'Well, let's get on with it!' attitude that surprised him every time he encountered it. He stopped at the bookcase and pulled out a book he'd noticed earlier, *Trauma in the Cancer Patient*. With Mrs James's file and Jack's paper it would make good reading on the plane.

'Mrs James had a fall,' Christa explained as they drove through the deserted streets. 'Like many country people they begin and finish the day early. Her husband thinks she got up to go to the bathroom. He doesn't know what time that was, but when he woke at ten and found she wasn't in bed he investigated and found her lying in the hall.'

Matt forgot about attitudes and concentrated on the patient.

'I bet the first thing he did was help her back to bed,' he muttered, and felt Christa's glance of surprise.

'I suppose he did,' she said. 'But if it was a simple slip and fall in her own home you wouldn't suspect spinal damage, surely.'

'Not usually,' Matt replied. 'But if she has had radiation therapy or has any bone metastases she could be at risk of bone fracture from the simplest of falls. Her husband is obviously concerned, which is why he contacted us.'

'He told Katie she's in a lot of pain, so much so he can't get her to answer any questions. He says her speech is unintelligible but she keeps talking. She's also showing signs of shock and is retching continuously.'

They reached the airport and raced across to the waiting plane.

'Three-quarters of an hour,' Eddie told them as they taxied along the brightly lit runway. Matt nodded and started reading.

'Found enough to keep you going?' Christa asked, as the change in the engine note signalled the end of their journey.

'Enough to know we should get her back to hospital as quickly as possible,' he told her. 'If she's bleeding internally or externally any blood product used for replacement needs to be considered in relation to her previous treatments. So many things can cause immunological reactions I'd prefer her oncologist ordered the blood products.'

Solar-powered batteries provided lights along the strip and Mr James was waiting for them, opening the doors of his sturdy farm vehicle as they approached with their paraphernalia.

'We might make a cup of tea while these two look at the patient,' Eddie suggested to Mr James after the worried man had driven them the short distance to the homestead and shown them into the bedroom.

Matt wondered if he was tactfully getting the man out of the way, and as he bent over the sick woman he understood her husband's concern. She lay on the bed, shivering and moaning. Tears trickled down her yellowy cheeks and sweat beaded her forehead. With frail, thin fingers she wiped ineffectually at her nose, then held the lace-trimmed handkerchief against her lips as she tried to hide another moan.

'She finished chemotherapy four weeks ago so she's well past the point where her bone marrow is most depressed and her blood count at its lowest,' he said to Christa, finishing his physical examination and coming back to inspect the venous access catheter tunnelling under the skin on the chest wall.

The woman's buttocks were bruised, and signs of bruising in the pelvic region worried him. Chemotherapy affected the body's blood-clotting mechanisms. Were the discolorations the result of the fall or something more sinister like DIC?

As he worked he talked quietly to the woman, asking questions she either did not understand or was too confused to answer. She flinched when he applied light pressure to her hips but she had also flinched when Christa took her pulse.

Christa reported her findings—pulse high and erratic and blood pressure low but within normal range. Reflexes in lower limbs fine. They smiled their relief at each other.

'I won't try to find a vein,' Matt said, knowing how often chemotherapy affected the integrity of the veins. 'I'll start a fluid infusion through the access catheter. She could have hypercalcemia, and I can run a large volume of fluid through it.'

He bent to unscrew the locked cap while Christa attached the intravenous tubing to the bag. Eddie appeared in the doorway with a much calmer Mr James.

'I'm concerned you might have damaged your hip or pelvis, Mrs James,' Matt explained, when the drip was running. 'I'm going to immobilise your legs.' He slid the padding they carried between them, then eased ties beneath her legs and bound them firmly together.

Eddie had carried the orthopaedic stretcher into the bedroom and Matt placed it on the bed beside the patient, then gave instructions to the two men to lift her while he stabilised the pelvic region with his hands. He secured her to the stretcher with chest, leg and head straps, leaving the pelvic area free, and signalled to the two men that they were ready to go.

The woman's moaning and distress was worsening and he remembered street kids he'd treated back in Paris. He opened his mouth to say, If I didn't know better, I'd say this was drug withdrawal, then cursed himself for a fool.

'Wait!' he said, opening Mrs James's file again. She was on slow-release morphine for pain at a dosage that made his mind boggle.

'Where are her tablets?' he asked Mr James, and followed the man down the hall. Had she forgotten to take one, which might explain a hasty walk down the darkened hall at night, or. . .

Mr James snapped on a light and revealed a shelf of medications a chemist would be proud to display in his shop.

'I don't know which is which,' he said, but Matt was already working his way along, lifting each bottle to read its properties and replacing it carefully.

He found the Roxanol bottle behind two other bottles, and wondered if she had hidden it from herself. Removing the cap, he shook out the contents—one remaining tablet. He thought of the pain killers he carried and realised that they would probably not be strong enough to manage the combined effects of acute pain and withdrawal the woman was suffering.

He filled a glass with water, then wondered about possible soft tissue and internal injuries. These were usually associated with pelvic fractures, but only because of the force the body would have to sustain to cause the injury to the joint. In this case, if the bones were damaged by either cancer or its treatment, a less forceful impact could shatter their fragility—without other injuries.

He'd better use parenteral pain relief anyway, he decided. There was no need to take added risks.

Within half an hour of landing they were in the air again. To Matt it always appeared as if time stopped while they were on the ground. Examination of the patient and preparation for transport seemed to take so long, yet every time he checked his watch as they took off again he was surprised to realise how quick they had been. He watched his patient, quieter since he'd given her morphine, and worried about the outcome.

If X-rays didn't show a fracture would they keep her in hospital? Would they try to ease her out of what had obviously become an addiction, or would they let her have whatever release she could find for however long she had left to live?

He sighed, glad he didn't have to be making those decisions. Much better to be doing what he could in an active way.

He thought of Caltura and knew that he was looking forward to returning there and working with Andrew Walsh. Then he thought of Lucia and sighed again.

He might tell himself he wouldn't fall in love with her, but he knew that it was already too late. She was as special to him as his mother had been to his father and he'd suspected that might be the case from the moment he met her.

So?

'Five minutes!'

Eddie's voice reminded the crew to fasten themselves in for landing, and Matt's attention switched back to his patient. He'd tried to contact her oncologist on the cellular phone but the man was away for a few days. Her medical records would be available at the hospital but Matt felt a strange reluctance to commit his suspicions to the file that would accompany her to Accident and Emergency.

'I'll go with her,' he said to Christa as they landed, and saw her nod.

'I'm glad,' she said, beginning the unstrapping procedure that would release their patient. 'Some things are too harsh when they're written down.'

It was after two before he left the hospital, having explained the suspected addiction and his fears about the blood products they might have to use. He'd been about to leave when he thought of his other 'patients' and he'd walked through the quiet wards to check on them. Earlier in the evening Karen, the German girl whose boyfriend had died, had been so emotionally over-wrought that she'd been sedated. He had watched her sleeping and thought again of Lucia.

Now, as he passed Aunt Steph's darkened house, he blew a kiss into the air. He was too tired to think, but somehow he would find a solution.

'Maybe it's fate doing me a favour by keeping us apart,' Lucia muttered to herself, arriving at work to hear of Jack's hospitalisation and Matt's second night on an emergency flight.

But it was her last personal thought. As if knowing they were short-staffed, the calls flowed in. Peter, on a clinic flight, handled all the early phone consultations but once he'd landed he was too busy and Matt was called in to take the steady stream of 'GP' work.

Lucia took him coffee and warmed at the smile in his eyes when he thanked her, but there was no time for conversation.

'I've found a locum who'll do phone and radio consultations, but no flights,' Leonie announced when Lucia went into the office to find the hospitalised patient files she needed to update.

'When does he start?' Lucia asked, hoping it meant that Matt could go home and get some sleep.

'Tomorrow.' Leonie frowned. 'I don't know whether I should cancel Matt's trip back to Caltura. We could still send the specialist and a nurse but—'

The phone interrupted her and she lifted the receiver, then smiled broadly at Lucia. Slipping a hand over the mouthpiece, she whispered to Lucia, 'I think he must have the place bugged!'

'Yes, Jack,' she said meekly, followed by, 'No, Jack, I wouldn't think of it. I've got Frank Wiley coming in so we'll manage and, no, I don't think you should come back Monday. Frank can give us all next week.'

She said goodbye and replaced the receiver, smiling slightly.

'Why was I worrying?' she asked Lucia. 'They operated on his abdomen, not his brain. It's ticking over as well as ever. I'm surprised he didn't ask for the phone consultations to be switched through to him at the hospital!'

'He probably hasn't thought of that yet,' Lucia said, and they both laughed.

'He rang to tell me Caltura's on, whatever else I have to sacrifice,' Leonie explained.

'Like Peter's and Matt's beauty sleep?'

'Something like that!'

They were interrupted by the noise of arrivals at the front door and Lucia walked out to investigate. An attractive couple in their mid-forties were hesitating in the foyer. She walked towards them, noticing, beneath healthy tans, the signs of strain and tiredness.

'May I help you?' she asked.

They turned towards each other, as if uncertain who would do the talking, then the man stepped forward and held out his hand.

'I am Schubert,' he said, shaking her hand firmly. 'And this is my wife. We wish to see the Flying Doctor.'

Schubert? One of the files she'd just retrieved had been a Schubert—one of the backpackers involved in the accident.

'Come this way,' she said, and led them into Leonie's office. Matt was busy and the radio room was no place for visitors at any time.

She introduced Leonie, waited while they agreed to coffee and left the room. On her way to the kitchen she looked into the radio room but Matt was talking and she didn't interrupt him.

It was an unwritten policy at the base to shield the flight staff from unnecessary intrusion. So many patients wanted to personally express their gratitude; so many grieving relatives wanted details of their loved one's death. Reporters sought gory accident details, while a few members of the general public wanted a vicarious thrill from hearing what had happened. The medical staff gave of their time whenever possible but in times of crisis it was hard.

She made coffee and took it into the office. Leonie was explaining what the flight crews had found, and how they had pieced together what had happened. She had the accident report on the desk in front of her but Lucia noticed that she didn't refer to it.

'But we wish to talk to the doctor who was at the accident,' the man insisted. 'We wish to hear this information from him, not you.'

It was arrogant rudeness, nothing less, Lucia thought as rage boiled up within her. She glanced at Leonie, who had clasped her hands together but showed no other reaction.

'One of the doctors is on an overnight clinic flight and won't return until late tomorrow evening,' she said calmly. 'I will give Dr Laurant the name of your hotel; I am sure he will contact you if he possibly can but we have one doctor off sick and Dr Laurant was called out to an emergency again last night. He does need to sleep some time,' she finished, less gently than she usually spoke.

Lucia busied herself serving coffee, admiring Leonie's tact as she switched the conversation to their daughter—asking if they had visited her and how she was progressing.

'Of course we're flying her straight home,' the man said, his English good enough to betray the patronisation in his voice. 'That doctor at the hospital said he had to stitch her wounds immediately to prevent infection, but the sooner she sees a real specialist the better.'

So much for a conversation switch, Lucia thought,

seeing Leonie's back straighten in anger.

'I'm sure she'll be happy to be back home with you,' Leonie replied and she sat very still, her knuckles showing white in the hands folded in front of her on the desk, while her guests drank their coffee.

'You will tell the doctor to phone us?' the man repeated as Leonie ushered them out of her office the moment the coffee was finished.

'Of course,' she assured him in a carefully neutral tone.

Lucia waited until they had departed, then turned to her boss.

'Will you tell Matt they want to see him?' she demanded. 'Will you let him waste his precious time on people like that?'

Leonie smiled at her, letting out her own pent-up breath in a deep sigh.

'You've got to realise they're upset,' she said. 'Their daughter's been injured; one of her friends has been killed, and they are in a foreign country. To get here in this time they must have left as soon as the police contacted them. They've been flying for thirty hours at least so, to them, it must seem as if they've come to the end of the earth!'

'You're too nice!' Lucia spluttered, her own anger at their attitude still bubbling within her. 'And Matt's too nice, too,' she added. 'He'll probably go along to the hotel and visit them, just so they can be rude to him as well!'

'I think that's up to him to decide,' Leonie said gently, and Lucia felt the heat wash colour into her cheeks.

She grabbed the files she'd extracted earlier and hurried back to her desk. Was her distress for Matt or

was it selfish? Was she upset because they were supposed to be going out?

She couldn't make decisions for Matt anyway! Last
night he'd asked her if she would consider going back
to France with him if they fell in love—became
lovers—and did not want to be parted at the end of the
year! So many 'ifs' so far down the track—all those
possibilities!

Yet she'd said no. Not in a word but it had been
implicit in her explanation. And his sadness when he'd
left her had been part sympathy for her but part sorrow
for what might have been between them.

Yet she couldn't accept his reasoning that they remain
as 'friends', although she'd been the one who had said
she would never have an affair with a doctor who was
just 'passing through'. But that had been back when
they'd first kissed—which seemed like years ago!

And now? She wanted him so badly that thinking
about him made her insides shake. She knew she should
be shocked for thinking this way or feel guilty because
even the thoughts were a betrayal of her friendship with
Anthony. But the desire to know Matt better was
stronger than any shame or guilt, and she couldn't
believe he didn't feel the same way. Couldn't accept
that it was better to have nothing than to share the magic
his kisses were promising. She had handled pain before:
surely she could cope with the pain of parting when it
happened.

In her mind Matt became the stumbling block.

For an adventurer he wasn't being very adventurous!
she decided crossly.

CHAPTER NINE

'MATT rang to say he wouldn't be able to take you out tonight. He has to meet the parents of one of the overseas visitors.' Aunt Steph was waiting at the top of the steps to tell her the bad news.

'He was still at the base when I left; he could have told me then,' Lucia replied ungraciously. 'And he doesn't *have* to meet those people.'

'Maybe it's a good thing. You sound as if you need an early night,' her aunt suggested.

'And what about Matt?' Lucia demanded. 'He's been called out the last two nights and in the office all day today doing phone consultations and now, when he should be sleeping, he's going to listen to these people harangue him and be rude about the Service and the hospital—'

She broke off when she realised that her aunt was chuckling.

'What's so funny?' she demanded, feeling angrier by the minute.

'You!' Aunt Steph replied. 'You can't decide whether you're mad at Matt because you're not going out or mad because he needs some sleep—which he wouldn't be getting anyway if you were going out with him.'

Lucia tried to make sense of the complicated sentence but decided that, after a day like today, it was beyond her.

'I'm going to have a bath,' she announced.

'Well, don't bother getting dressed for the hospital,' Aunt Steph called after her. 'I've done your visit for today.'

Lucia turned, regarding her erratic relative in astonishment.

'You've done my visit?' she repeated, and saw the dark head nod.

'Why?'

Her aunt walked towards her and took her shoulders.

'It has been good for you to have the interest—up until now,' she said softly. 'And there's no reason why you can't continue to see your special patients once or twice a week—but not every night, Lucia. You have Matt's company for a short time—enjoy it. Be young. Besides, I enjoyed my visit today—far more than I would have imagined possible. They are such characters—your friends up there.'

'But how did you know which people were RFDS patients?'

'I saw Carol at the hostel first,' she explained, and Lucia remembered that Carol had visited her aunt a few times while she was at work. 'She took me up and introduced me to the receptionist and explained I would be visiting, then she showed me all the wards and I met the people who are already in there.'

'Even the accident victims?' Lucia's amazement at her aunt's behaviour was clear in her incredulous tone.

'Oh, yes,' Aunt Steph said blithely. 'I sat with a lovely blonde girl, Karen, for a long time. She was so sad because her boyfriend was killed, but I told her all about you and Daniel and how you grieved and how, out of the blue, Matt came along and now you are happy again.'

Lucia opened and shut her mouth a few times before she could make a sound, and when the words did come they rasped across her constricted vocal chords.

'You talked about all that?' she demanded, unable to believe her aunt—or any of her family—had ever given her embryonic relationship with Daniel more than a passing thought. They had known she grieved for him as a playmate and friend—but as her love?

'It seemed to help,' her aunt said, 'and I promised I'd go back tomorrow to sit with her again, although I believe her parents are on their way. You have your bath and get into something comfortable. We'll have dinner and lounge around in front of the television until it's not too early to go to bed!'

Lucia obeyed, turning back towards her bedroom and the connecting bathroom. She was trying to assimilate too much information at once, she told herself when her brain refused to accommodate the sudden changes in her life.

But what if Matt didn't want to spend time with her— after she'd explained why she couldn't leave Australia? What would she do in the evenings now that her aunt had taken over the job that made her feel busy and useful and less lonely than she had been in the beginning?

He rang as she dried herself and she stood, towel-draped, in the bedroom, looking out over the lush green jungle of her aunt's back yard and trembling at the sound of his voice.

Is it love or lust that makes me feel this way? she wondered, barely listening to his apologetic explanations.

'But Karen's the blonde girl, the one whose boyfriend died,' she told him when enough of the conversation had registered to make a little bit of sense. 'It's not her parents who've come. It's Lucilla's.'

She heard his tiredness in the little sigh that trickled down the line and instantly felt guilty about her own disappointment.

'Karen's parents have also arrived,' he explained, 'and have met up with the Swiss couple at the hotel. I've agreed to meet with all of them—for a short time only.' He paused and she waited, not allowing herself to hope. 'Then I really must get some sleep,' he finished, his exhaustion, like an amorphous entity, coming at her over the wires. 'I'm sorry, Lucia!'

'You don't have to apologise,' she told him gruffly. 'You need sleep more than anything. I'm just sorry you have to spend some of your precious free time with these people.' She hesitated for a moment and added, 'But I can understand that you feel you must. You wouldn't be the person—' she bit back the 'I love' which nearly escaped '—you are if you didn't feel that way.'

The cancelled dinner arrangement set the pattern for the week. With only two doctors available for flights, days off were cancelled and both Peter and Matt remained on call.

'I miss you,' he murmured when they met one morning in the lunch-room. He was unshaven, his eyes red-rimmed from lack of sleep, and so exhausted-looking that Lucia longed to take him in her arms and hold him against her—to will some of her energy into him.

Instead she smiled and said, 'Long night?' knowing he would hear the sympathy in her voice.

'Another one,' he agreed, with a faint reminder of

his wonderful smile. 'There's been a gastro-enteritis outbreak at Caltura. Andrew Walsh has set up a mini-hospital for all the young children and babies in the old schoolhouse. He ran a lead from the shop so he could shift the radio in there, and has been nursing his patients with instructions from me for the last six hours.'

'He radioed in at three in the morning about a gastro outbreak?' Lucia asked, her anger, too close to the surface where Matt was concerned, rising again.

Tired though he was, his smile widened.

'I was speaking to him earlier in the night. The medical chest had become depleted. With no health worker, no one was taking responsibility for it and re-ordering supplies. All he could do was boil water and mix a little salt and sugar in it and use that for fluid replacement. At three o'clock I woke up thinking of something so, knowing he wouldn't be sleeping much, I contacted him. As it turned out, he'd been about to radio us. He's very worried about two of the children.'

Pride swelled in her heart and she wanted to hug him so badly that her arms ached.

'So what's happening?'

'Christa's on her way out there. She's taking drugs and electrolyte replacement powders to restock the chest and start a store of supplies. She's also got IV fluids, and if Andrew can administer them she'll leave some with him. Then she'll bring back the children who need hospitalisation. Although it sounds a lot of work it doesn't need a doctor and the flight should be a straight-forward evacuation.'

'And can you go home now?' she asked. 'Who's on duty?'

'Peter's on a clinic flight, Frank's coming in at ten

and I'm going home to bed as soon as he gets here.'
He ticked their movements off on his slender fingers.

Lucia watched with a strange fascination. Tired as he
was, the waves of awareness seemed just as strong and
the words 'to bed' echoed like a taunting refrain in her
mind. She looked up and found him watching her; looking into her eyes! And for a moment she thought she
saw the desire she felt mirrored in their blueness.

Don't be ridiculous, she told herself, and tried to
recall what they'd been talking about.

'But you'll still be on call?'

He nodded.

'Bad week, huh?' he said, and when she agreed he
added, 'Well, at least it didn't happen on my first week
here. I don't think I could have stood the shock of going
straight from a life of leisure to this pace!'

She smiled, pleased that he could still joke about the
situation.

'Shall I make you coffee? I'm getting Leonie her
second cup for the day,' she explained, remembering
why she was in the room.

He shook his head and reached out to run one finger
up her arm. The touch jolted her body to life and the
air around them arced with an electric force.

'I've a report to write up before I go home,' he said
softly, and she knew she was imagining the seduction
she heard in the everyday words. 'I caught a glimpse
of you heading this way and wanted to see you, if only
for a few minutes.'

She wasn't imagining it! Lucia felt relief swamp her
body and she smiled. It was going to be all right! She
was certain of that.

'Come up this evening if you're awake and not called

out,' she suggested, and wondered if she was pushing beyond the undefined boundaries of their relationship. 'Or any evening,' she added, hoping to make the invitation sound less pushy.

'I'll try,' he promised, and turned away and walked out of the room, leaving Lucia puzzling over too many things.

Was the timing of this crisis good or bad? Matt wondered as he walked back to his desk. He had only to hear Lucia's voice from somewhere in the building, or catch sight of her petite figure as she whisked about her work, to know that he still wanted her. But it was not the thought of a lustful satisfaction that absorbed all his free minutes but the strange possessiveness he felt towards her, an overpowering new emotion that he thought was probably love—an impossible love!

'I'm sorry, Matt, it's Andrew again. You wouldn't believe it, but now he's got a fellow come in with what sounds like a heart attack, as well as his sick babies.' Katie sounded anxious, even over the scratchy internal phone.

'I'll be right there,' he assured her, and hurried back to the radio room.

As he picked up the radio mouthpiece he said a silent prayer of thanks that it was someone as unflappable as Andrew at the other end. Most normally calm people, given the deteriorating circumstances, would be edging towards hysteria by this time.

'Can you give me his symptoms?' he asked, and listened while Andrew began to describe what he'd seen and been told.

'He's very sweaty, shivering, grey-looking,' he said.

'Says the pain in his chest is terrible but he's rubbing his left arm more than his chest. Says he's sure he's going to die but he wants to throw up first.'

And that's a very neat précis of symptoms for a myocardial infarction, Matt thought.

'The plane must be nearly there,' he reminded Andrew. 'Lie the fellow down, keep him warm and reassure him. Give him two aspirins now. I'll try to get on to Christa and explain what's happened. She can try a glyceryl trinitrate tablet under his tongue within minutes of arriving. If he came straight to you when the pain started he's got a good chance, but while Christa's dealing with him you'll have to get the kids you want transported back here all ready to go.'

'You're saying you want that plane turned around and out of here as quickly as possible,' Andrew clarified.

'Exactly! Christa will set up an IV line. If the pain isn't reduced by the sublingual tablet she'll use morphine and an IV infusion of NTG. But if we can get him to hospital, where they can start thrombolytic therapy within six hours, he'll have a much better chance.'

He heard Andrew speak to someone and waited until the muted conversation finished.

'I've three helpers here,' he explained. 'I was giving orders about the aspirin to my staff!' Matt grinned, pleased that Andrew could still joke after the night he'd endured.

'See if you can find the local copy of the man's file,' he told Andrew. 'Christa will need to check it and ask him some questions about his general health. The thrombolytic drugs can cause bleeding so if there's any reason you know why he shouldn't have it—recent surgery, history as a bleeder, recent head injury, liver dysfunction—tell Christa.'

'I've found most of the old files so I'll see if he's got one. He's a healthy looking fifty-year-old,' Andrew explained. 'He certainly hasn't had surgery since I've been here. He's one of the stockmen who works full time on the cattle property the Caltura community runs half an hour's drive from here. Good worker, from all accounts.'

'Then he has a good chance of recovery,' Matt promised. 'The fitter he was before the incident, the better his body will cope.'

'Plane's coming now,' Andrew said, then he added, 'Thanks for everything, mate,' before signing off.

Matt felt a glow of satisfaction. He knew 'mate' was a common substitute for a man's name in Australia, but Andrew's use of the word had a special significance. It was an acceptance, a sign of a special friendship, a word that meant he 'belonged'.

Frank Wiley arrived and tapped him on the shoulder, waking him from a reverie that was close to sleep.

'Home to bed, youngster,' Frank ordered, and Matt smiled.

'You bet!' he said, using another Australianism he'd picked up in his travels. 'But first I'd better fill you in.'

He described what was happening out at Caltura, then added, 'The plane's landing now and the mobile phone is out of range, so if Christa doesn't contact you within the next three-quarters of an hour I think you should call Caltura and check that everything's under control.'

Frank nodded. 'Things often happen in threes. It would be just our luck to find she's arrived there and

some blighter's been bitten by a snake, or a baby's
decided it's time to be born.'

He smiled at Matt.

'You go home and rest, Matt,' he said. 'I was doing
this kind of thing while you were in nappies. It's a bit
of interest in my retirement now, filling in like this, but
I haven't forgotten how to use the radio and I keep
abreast of all the latest treatment and technology so I
can still be useful when I'm needed.'

Matt smiled at the older man.

'You'd have some stories to tell,' he suggested, thinking of the old planes and the basic equipment that the
RFDS had used in the past.

A call prevented Frank from answering but Matt
knew that he would talk to the older man again soon.
The special magic of the Service was taking hold of his
soul, and he hungered to know more of its history and
to hear the tales of the early days.

He walked through the building where the rituals of
the day were under way, slowing as he passed Lucia's
desk. She was speaking, low-voiced, into the phone and
her head was bent over a file as she wrote a message
from whoever was at the other end.

His fingers tingled with an urge to brush across her
dark, curling hair, but he knew that if he touched her,
even lightly and in passing, it would not be enough.

It would start the ache again, he reminded himself,
striding to the door and pushing out into the enveloping
warmth. Or bring it back to fierce and painful life, for
it was always there. It was a physical longing like
nothing he had ever known before, and some instinct
told him it was never going to go away.

As he reached number sixty-four he paused, looking

up the road towards Aunt Steph's house. As soon as life settled down again at the base, maybe he should go out with Peter and some of his medical friends. Maybe seeing other women might rationalise his feelings for Lucia.

He pushed open the gate then kicked it shut, swinging at it with his leg while his mind used a similar mental movement to toss aside his 'maybe' thought.

'If you ever get any free time again, Matthieu Laurant,' he told himself as he walked around the main house to his flat, 'I can't imagine either common sense or rationalisation will stop you spending it with Lucia!'

It had to be love, he thought gloomily. But there are oceans and continents between Australia and France, not just a narrow channel! He showered and fell into bed, where images of a dark-haired beauty soon lulled him into a dreamless sleep.

By Saturday Lucia had become resigned to brief, too-public meetings at the base and snatched moments when Matt would return from a late flight and come up the road to sit on the front steps and hold her in his arms for a few minutes before seeking the sleep he so desperately needed.

He would tell her about his day, running his fingers through her hair, then kiss her gently on the lips and walk wearily away. The attraction was still there, she knew, but at the moment it was blanketed by Matt's professionalism and her own concern for his health. He needed sleep far more than he needed sex, she reminded herself one night, and blushed to think she had entertained such a wayward idea!

Yet she knew the embers of desire still smouldered,

banked down but generating more and more heat in the dark, deep corners of their sensual selves.

She went to the amphitheatre with Aunt Steph while Matt flew through the swirling cloud masses of a tropical low to bring out a panicky pregnant woman before the weather made it impossible for her to travel. She walked on the beach alone on Sunday while he slept, then ate the baked dinner she'd prepared herself while he flew to the hospital at Castleford, where a rodeo accident had left one of the local boys with a suspected cervical spine fracture.

'And this week's going to be just as bad. Tomorrow he goes back to Caltura,' she explained to Aunt Steph over roast potatoes so perfect they seemed to melt in the mouth once the outside, crispy crust was bitten through. 'Two days there, on duty Wednesday and a two-day clinic flight Thursday and Friday.'

'It's his work,' Aunt Steph pointed out.

'I know,' Lucia groaned. 'And he loves it.'

'He would be a different person if he did it purely as his duty,' her aunt said softly. 'And would you love that person?' Lucia groaned again, too confused to be surprised by her aunt's assumption.

'What do I know about love?' she demanded. 'I can't decide if I love the person he is, Aunt Steph, let alone make comparisons with a duty-orientated Matt. And the whole situation is hopeless, anyway,' she finished. 'Perhaps it would be better if he's kept as busy as this for the whole twelve months, then I won't be tempted to do something I might regret later.'

The words were out before she realised what she was saying and she looked up, aghast at what she had said, to see how her aunt had reacted.

Aunt Steph smiled, and Lucia saw a flicker of girlish beauty and a flash of pain before her features settled back into their usual calm, contemplative mould.

'You must make your own decisions,' she said quietly, 'but remember this. You can regret not doing something just as much as you can regret doing it.' She paused, as if to allow Lucia to assimilate what she was saying, and added, 'Remember, if you decide to hold back you won't have even the memories to hold in your heart when today is yesterday and the nights are long and lonely.'

Lucia sat and stared at her, feeling the pain coming in waves from her beloved relative.

'Who. . .?' she began, but Aunt Steph held up her hand, rose from the table and walked out of the kitchen.

Shock! That's what it was, Lucia decided as she cleared the table and washed the dishes with hands that trembled constantly. Shock that her aunt—her surrogate mother—was virtually telling her to go ahead and have an affair with Matt.

She tidied away the last plate and looked around. Beneath the shock was an indefinable sadness for her aunt's lost dreams and, layered even lower, a tentative excitement mixed through with trepidation. Walking through the quiet house, past the thin line of light beneath Aunt Steph's bedroom door, she sat down on the front steps and thought for a while then nodded decisively and made her way back to her bedroom where she phoned Anthony.

'I knew he was seeing a bit of Gloria before you went away,' her mother said when she poured out her surprise at Anthony's reaction to her call in a second telephone call a little later. 'It was one of the reasons I

wanted you to go. You'd turned to each other when
Daniel died and comforted each other, but it would have
been a mistake to persuade yourselves that friendship
might turn into love.'

'Aunt Steph said something like that,' Lucia admitted,
'but I felt you all expected something to come of it.'

'I'm sure Anthony's parents will learn to love Gloria
as much as they love you,' her mother said tactfully.

She talked for another twenty minutes before hanging
up, feeling more at ease than she had for a long time.
She had taken a small step forward along the road to her
long-delayed independence and tomorrow, after work,
she'd see the GP up the road and take another step. Just
in case!

Jack, tired and pale, returned to work on Wednesday
and the hectic pace eased.

'Go home and get some sleep,' Jack ordered at noon.
Matt looked up from the Caltura files he was still trying
to reduce to manageable order and grinned at him.

'Sleep? What's that? Will I get it at the supermarket?'

Lucia, walking past, heard their voices and looked
around in time to see Jack cuff Matt lightly on the head.

'Now!' he ordered, closing the file on Matt's desk
and putting a dolphin-shaped paperweight on top of it.

'Nearly now,' Matt agreed, and held up his hands as
Jack leaned threateningly towards him. 'I'll go, I'll go.'

Jack smiled at him and as he walked back to the radio
room Matt stood up, stretched and winked at Lucia.

'Race you to the equipment room,' he whispered,
then he crossed the space between them, grasped her
hand and tugged her into the small storeroom where he
had first kissed her.

'Just one minute!' he murmured, holding her in his arms. 'One minute of peace!'

Lucia held him, breathing in the smell of him, absorbing the warmth of him and feeling the lean hard muscle of him.

'I'm going home to sleep without a pager to disturb me or call me out again. I will set my alarm clock for five o'clock, get up, shower and shave and make myself as handsome as I can and present myself at your wondrous aunt's place at six. Do you want to go out to eat to make up for all the missed occasions or will we go back to our old routine?'

She pressed her face into the hollow of his neck.

'Let's eat at home, go up to the hospital and walk back in the darkness hand in hand.' The words tumbled off her lips as her heart cavorted. The repetition of their early rituals might restore some order and balance to the chaotic excitement rioting through her mind and body.

She felt him nod and his arms tightened momentarily before he dropped a kiss on her cheek and left the room, leaving her to reach out for the shelving to support her weak-kneed body.

He was there at six and looked as she had first seen him in the garden at the base. He was rested, his skin gleaming from his shower and shave and his eyes dancing with delight as she twirled in front of him on the front veranda.

'I bought a new dress to celebrate your return to a near-normal life, and Aunt Steph has cooked her special crab lasagne.'

She took his hand to lead him through to the kitchen but the potency of the sensory magic between them struck her senses like a lightning bolt, and she stood, stock-still while her blood boiled and fizzed and her nerves jangled with the overwhelming urgency of her need.

'I wrote away on Wednesday, requesting information on studying ophthalmology in Australia,' he said, very clearly and concisely, although she knew he was shaking as much as she was.

He would stay in Australia? Do that for her? The words were the sweetest she had ever heard—a gift more precious than she would ever have dreamed he could provide.

And what can I give him? she wondered. Then she knew. She would tell him of her own decision—a decision that had not been dependent on a promise of for ever from him.

She turned so that she was facing him and looking into the eyes that were waiting expectantly for her reaction.

'I went to the doctor for a prescription for the pill,' she replied, ignoring the heat rushing through her body which must be turning her cheeks scarlet with embarrassment. 'On Monday.'

CHAPTER TEN

THEY stood and looked at each other, holding hands but otherwise not touching, until Aunt Steph's call to dinner brought them out of their other world.

'We'll talk later,' Matt whispered, his voice hoarse with emotion. He led her around the veranda to the kitchen. 'I don't want to rush you, Lucia, into something you might regret later.'

Lucia smiled, wishing she could tell him what her aunt had said about regret!

'We'll talk later,' she echoed, following him into the kitchen on feet that seemed to float a foot above the ground.

Afterwards Lucia tried to recall the meal, or their conversation, or anything—but all she could remember was sitting next to Matt, their knees touching beneath the table and her blood singing of her love.

They walked hand in hand to the hospital, talking of work and everyday things, putting off the moment when they would move into each other's arms and free the forces that were escalating within their bodies.

'Would you like to get engaged?' Matt asked as they entered the well-lit hospital grounds.

Lucia stopped abruptly.

'I don't need a commitment,' she said. 'You said yourself that the physical thing between us might fizzle out and we might part as friends.'

She studied his face, desperate to read what he was

thinking, but for once no hint of his emotions lurked there and she felt lost and very alone. 'And if it doesn't stop we have an option if you could study here. Why should I need more commitment than that?'

She couldn't tell if he was relieved or disappointed but her own jolting panic when he mentioned an engagement had forced her to protest. It was all too new! And, having cut herself off from all adolescent experimentation in her teenage years, she knew little of relationships between men and women.

He shook his head and smiled, and relief swamped her. It was going to be all right!

'You could ask for the stars and be given them, Lucia, yet you want so little,' he murmured, and slipped an arm around her shoulders and walked her towards the hospital.

'I'm going up to see Remi,' he told her, and Lucia remembered that he was the second man who had been in Intensive Care. 'He's in a normal ward now and will be transferred south tomorrow.'

'The last of your accident victims to go?'

He nodded.

'Yes. Lucilla went immediately, of course, and Karen's parents arranged transport for her, Julie and Georg. They will all make better recoveries than we had originally hoped, but it still makes me feel sad to think their great adventure was cut short like that.'

'Some great adventure if they intended taking Lucilla all the way!' Lucia reminded him, and saw his smiling response. She wriggled a little closer to his body, more at ease in this 'good friends' situation than she was in the desire-charged atmosphere of their attraction.

'I'll finish up with Mrs James,' he continued. 'Have you visited her?'

'Only once,' Lucia explained. 'Since Aunt Steph took over the visiting I must admit I've been very slack. I still see Carol most days, of course, but the others. . .'

'Perhaps you've had other things on your mind,' he teased, and brushed his lips across her hair before releasing her at the doorway into the hospital. 'Meet you right here later,' he promised as he waited for her to walk through the door, and the thrill of excitement she thought had died surged through her once again.

Would it be tonight? Would they go back to his place? What would it be like. . .?

He must have sensed her hesitation for he took her hand again and drew her back outside, finding a shadowy corner behind one of the huge entrance pillars.

'I won't rush you into anything, Lucia,' he said, his voice so low and husky that it made her knees shake. 'Whatever happens will happen because we both want it, and you will know when the time is right.'

He leant forward and kissed her very gently on the lips, then drew her hand through the crook of his elbow and rested it on his arm. Thus escorted, she entered the hospital, still shaking but sure of his support and understanding.

They walked home beneath a magic moon, full-blown and golden yellow, still low in the eastern sky. They talked of the people they had visited but the silent message that passed between their fingers hastened their footsteps until they drew into the deep shadows of Aunt Steph's garden and could ease the ache of longing in each other's arms.

It began with kisses, deep and searching—pledges of a mutual need that words could not define. Lucia felt the heat sweep through her body and pressed closer, seeking relief from a pain she could not understand—so delicious, so tantalising, so sharp and demanding was it.

Then Matt's hands began exploring her body, running lightly across bare skin and slithery clothing, feeling her curves and softness and lingering here, teasing there, making her tremble with urgency and shudder with delight.

Her hands moved of their own accord, tentative at first then bolder, making discoveries of their own. His spine was straight and hard beneath his skin but at its base there must have been a sensitive spot for he groaned against her mouth as her fingers dug in hard, pressing his body closer to hers and sliding along the tiny joined bones.

Then his hand slipped between their bodies and brushed against her breast, and it was her turn to groan for the lightest of touches sent a sheet of flame from her nipple to her. . .?

She didn't know the word, although names she'd only read in magazines jostled in her mind.

Could a part of her body she'd always regarded as purely functional take on a life of its own?

Matt's hand lingered on her breast, his fingers rubbing then plucking at her nipple, and she knew the answer. The ache between her thighs intensified, the desire burning there so strong and deep that she wondered if it could ever be quenched.

She moved against him and the hardness she felt excited her even more; her breath came in gasps and words were impossible. His fingers left her breast and brushed across her stomach, then slipped between her legs and cupped the seat of her tortuous delight, stroking so gently while the tremors in her body grew and grew.

And if he can generate such delight touching me, can I do the same for him? The question sounded in her ears, although conscious thought had not produced it. She shifted slightly and and allowed her hand to explore his body, to touch—so very lightly and half-embarrassed—the straining heat of his desire pressed against his lightweight cotton trousers.

'This is teasing, my love,' he murmured, lifting his head so the air brushed against her swollen, sensitised lips. 'And torture!'

He groaned again and pressed his hand on top of her so-tentative one, moulding it to the shape of his erection so that she could feel the heat and throbbing need he held in check.

'Shall we go to your flat?' she asked, knowing that he would let her set the pace but still uncertain; wanting him, yet hesitant, suddenly aware of how little she knew about sex and how much she might reveal of her inexperience.

'Would you stay?' he asked, the words rasping out of his throat as if his neck were gripped by strangling hands.

'Aunt Steph—work—I don't know,' she faltered, and he put his arms around her shoulders and hugged her tightly.

'I don't want our first time together to be a quick or furtive thing, Lucia,' he explained. 'I want to make it right for you—a special memory to be treasured for ever. And I'd like it to end in our sleeping in each other's arms and waking together to make love again.'

She nodded, disappointed now that the decision had been taken away from her although she should have been glad.

'I have this weekend off,' he whispered, 'and I'm told there's a wonderful beach resort just north of here with cabins beneath the palm trees and soft, yellow sand leading down to a crystal clear sea.'

He tilted her head so that she could look up at the moon, silvery now it had lost the feverish redness of the setting sun.

'That moon is too good to waste, isn't it, my love? Would you come away with me?'

She took a deep breath, knowing the commitment she was about to make would change her life for ever.

'I'll come away with you, Matt,' she whispered, and in her heart she felt an ease that told her that it was time for change, for growing up beyond the shadows of yesterday and for gathering the memories of tomorrow.

Telling Aunt Steph was easy compared to the difficulty of getting through two more days at work and pretending all the time that nothing momentous was about to happen in her life. Fortunately Matt was on the clinic flight. He had left early Thursday and would not be back until Friday evening, but while he was away he would phone the rental company to arrange to hire a car, and they would leave early on Saturday.

But would Saturday ever come?

Lucia packed and repacked the small bag she was taking, blushing when she thought of Matt seeing her undressed and hugging her body as she tried to control the electrifying excitement that even thinking of him engendered.

By the time they drove north she was too tense to speak and she suspected that the tremors that were shaking her body were matched by a trembling in his. As they rounded a headland and looked down on the cove where the resort nestled he steered the car off the road and stopped.

Reaching out, he took her hand in his and ran his fingers across her palm.

'I'm so happy I can barely breathe,' he admitted, 'but coming with me doesn't commit you to anything. You understand that, Lucia.'

He sounded so uncertain that her own ambivalence vanished and she leant across and kissed him on the lips.

'If I seem doubtful it's because. . .well. . .'

She looked at him, eyes beseeching help, then blurted out, 'I've never done this before. I might disappoint you!'

He smiled, then chuckled and drew in a breath so deep she could see his chest expand.

'Nothing you could ever do would disappoint me, my Lucia,' he murmured and with fingers linked, he slid the car back into gear and they drove down to the resort.

They were shown into a thatched cabin and, as Matt had promised, it was shaded by coconut palms, with sand beyond the front door and green translucent water beckoning to them beyond the beach.

The huge bed seemed to dominate the room and Lucia's apprehension rose again but Matt closed the door behind the friendly maid and took her in his arms, kissing away her fear and rekindling the embers deep in her body.

'Let's swim, sunbathe and swim again,' he suggested, whispering the words so seductively into her ear that she felt the tremors begin again.

She glanced across his shoulder at the bed and smiled when he said, 'It will still be there later, Lucia. It's not going anywhere.' He pushed her a little away from his body and looked down into her eyes. 'We are here for a relaxing weekend remember, not a sexual marathon.'

She smiled uncertainly but when he steered her towards the bathroom and handed her the little bag she'd packed so many times, saying, 'Change into your swimming costume. I'll meet you on the beach,' she relaxed and whipped out the black and white bikini she'd bought yesterday and slipped into it, anxious to be with him again.

They swam and sunbaked, Matt sleeping deeply until Lucia woke him, anxious that he'd burn. They swam again, frolicking in the water like two children let loose from school. Tensions drained away but the desire between them was heightened by the fleeting contact of their slick, wet bodies, yet held in check, building to an exquisite agony.

'Race you back to the cabin,' Matt challenged when they knew the sun was too high in the sky for safe sunbathing.

Lucia ran from the water, scooped up her towel and raced across the now-burning sand.

Matt overtook her and she saw the water gleaming on his chest and catching, diamond-like, in the curling hairs of his legs.

Her breathing slowed, then speeded up as her heart

began thumping in her chest. She tried to run but faltered and would have fallen but he was there and scooped her up into his arms, carrying her easily into the cool gloom of the cabin and placing her with infinite tenderness down on the bed.

He knelt above her and dropped a kiss onto her salty lips before his mouth moved away, across her chin and down towards her breasts. She held her breath and waited, her body tensing, wanting and not wanting the delicious torture she knew instinctively his mouth could inflict.

His lips touched one nipple, and she cried out. Her hands grasped his head, not knowing if she wanted it to stay there or to move away. He shifted, settling on his side beside her, and again his lips brushed hers, still softly, while the fingers of one hand continued teasing at her breast, building up an urgency that made her want to cry out.

He slid his hand lower, touching skin and sweeping at the droplets of water, brushing across the satiny bikini pants and starting up a throbbing response within her.

Now his lips were more demanding and the exploratory hand, as if acting under its own will, was torching her body to life with tiny caresses and intimate demands. As Matt's kisses deepened she felt the fingers once again at her breast, felt them slip beneath the wet material and tease at the nubbly point of her contracted nipple. She moved beneath the tormenting hand, her back arching as it sought relief.

As if drawn by her movement, the teasing fingers moved lower and slid beneath the concealing costume to touch the softness of her and draw moisture from her being.

She shuddered at the shocking intimacy and again at the delight of her reaction. Her lips opened as she gasped aloud and his tongue took advantage, plundering her mouth and drawing forth a passionate response. His body was warm at her side but she knew she wanted more and, when he stopped the kisses and once again slid his lips across her breast, she cried out at the searing desire his mouth and fingers were provoking. Her mind had ceased to work and she could only feel, and enjoy, and respond to the magic of Matt's caresses.

Then somehow they were both undressed and he moved to lie closer so that skin met skin, fanning the flaring heat of awareness higher and higher. As his fingers drew responses from the sensitive tissues of her body her own strayed to hold him, marvelling at the satiny fullness and excited by an age-old knowledge that seemed to settle over her—a feeling of rightness that relaxed all fears.

He paused in his tender ministrations for a moment, moving and whispering about taking no chances and not long enough on the pill, then his fingers found her moist readiness and, easing the ready lips apart, he thrust into her body, making her want to cry out with a triumphant fulfilment.

He withdrew and thrust again, murmuring love and reassurance, his body moving over hers in such a way that the curling mist of hair on his chest still tantalised her breasts and made her move against him, arching to accept his fullness. There was a momentary sharpness and a sense of shock then the rhythm changed and she was lulled into a gentle rocking motion, warm and safe, that built up again faster and faster, a new tension carrying her higher and higher.

Her thighs stiffened and muscles she did not know existed tightened in her body, clinging to him, drawing him in and in, on and on, until she was carried high above the earth into an unknown realm of glory. Then she cried out and clung to him as her body came apart and melted, and shudders of sensation ran down to tingle in her toes.

His shoulders tensed and she felt an answering shudder in his muscles before he, too, lay still, quiescent in her arms, a weight so dear she wanted him to lie there always, pinning her to reality after she'd lost all control and been lifted to another world.

'I love you, Lucia,' he murmured against her cheek, and twisted onto his side, drawing her with him so that they lay with legs entwined, still joined, cocooned in the special ambience of mutual pleasure.

It was a weekend of pleasure that sated Lucia's senses. Time and time again they made love, climbing together to the peak of ecstasy and pushing to the limits of sensory delight, until she would collapse and lie, weak and reeling with a momentous fatigue, in Matt's sheltering arms.

They drove home, her hand resting on his thigh, his eyes, when he turned to look at her, alight with the love he'd pledged so often over the past forty-eight hours.

Then the real world intruded and Matt, on call on Sunday night, was summoned to work soon after they returned. It was a radio consultation but when he didn't phone her by ten o'clock she knew that she wouldn't see him that night and he was gone, back to Caltura for

the regular clinic flight, before Lucia arrived at work
on Monday.

The time they had together became doubly precious,
shared moments of quiet camaraderie as well as heated
exchanges of their physical passion. When he was home
they spent their time in his flat, or on Aunt Steph's
veranda, needing to be alone together with no intrusion
from the outside world.

With Matt away so often from the base, Lucia imagined that their delight in each other was still a secret so
she was surprised, weeks later, when Peter stopped by
her desk.

'He'll be back tomorrow,' he said, an unfamiliar
gentleness in his voice.

She looked up, startled from a dream of Matt, her
eyes asking a hundred questions.

'Foolish child!' he chided, one finger flicking carelessly in her curls. 'Did you really think you could skip
about the corridors and blush and sparkle when you met
each other in the lunch-room or emerge all rosy from
the equipment room without anyone noticing?'

Lucia felt the colour crawling into her cheeks, pushed
by the heat of embarrassment that was enveloping her
body. She looked up at Peter, unable to deny, unable
to reply!

'Don't be afraid to show it, Lucia,' he said gravely.
'Love is always beautiful and first love so special you
must hold it close to you and nurture it like a fragile
plant that needs giving and sharing and caring and com-
passion in order to survive.'

'That's exactly how it feels, Peter,' she whispered,
amazed that he, of all the staff, should zero in on the

secret fears behind the wondrous love. 'It's like a beautiful illusion or a brightly coloured bubble—too precious
to last, too wonderful to really be mine to keep for ever.'

'Even if it's not for ever, hold on to it now,' he told
her, then patted her on the head and walked away, leaving Lucia gazing bemusedly after him.

The bubble burst a month later—burst and shattered,
its kaleidoscope of colour ripped apart by capricious
fate. But its bursting scattered tears and anguish and
left in its wake a heaviness of defeat on all the staff at
the base. It was pricked by a phone call for Matt to tell
him the worst of news. Jack took the message and waited
at the base, in Leonie's office, to tell him. Matt,
returning from a mission where he'd saved a life, was
told of one he'd lost.

'Your father was struck down by a speeding car,'
Jack told him, while Lucia stroked his fingers and held
out her arms to comfort him as the cry of denial rose
from his lips.

They waited until his shoulders stopped their heaving
and his breathing steadied. When his face asked the
questions he could not voice Jack explained about the
late-night call to the hospital, how staff had seen his
father leave then seen the lights and heard the cry and
found him already dead a minute later.

'They tried to revive him, Matt, but he'd been thrown
against the raised edge of the pavement.' Jack said no
more, knowing that Matt's training would supply
the rest.

'I must phone home,' he said, his voice so hoarse
that Lucia didn't recognise it. 'My mother, sisters. . .
me not there. . .'

Jack dialled the number and handed the receiver to
Matt. Lucia moved away but his hand clung to hers and
she pushed him into Leonie's chair and knelt beside
him, kneading at his fingers as she silently conveyed
her sympathy.

Jack dropped them home, hours later, at Aunt Steph's
house and Lucia took him into her bedroom and
undressed him, knowing that shock was shaking through
his body and that sleep might blot out some of the pain.
She lay holding him through the night and seeing all
her dreams dying—one by one.

He would fly south in the morning and wait there for
the first available flight to Paris. In her heart of hearts
she knew that this was goodbye.

At dawn he stirred, waking up to memories too hor-
rible to bear, and shuddered and cried in her arms. When
the storm had passed he slipped out of her narrow bed
and she heard him showering. By the time he reappeared
calm and composed, she knew he had regained the
strength he would need to get him home.

He sat down on the bed and took his hand in hers,
looking down at her with eyes aged by grief.

'I won't be able to come back, my love,' he whispered. 'My mother. . .my sisters still so young. . .
They'll need a man around the place; someone to take
care of them. . . Oh, Lucia!'

The double anguish bit into her soul and she clung
to him, crying herself yet knowing what he said was
true. His family would be needing him and his place
was there—at least until his sisters finished school and
were ready to take control of their own lives. If anyone
knew about families and need she did, she thought,

bitterness touching places that had only ever experienced love.

'I know you can't come, precious girl. I know your own commitments but maybe—surely—we will meet again.' He lifted his ravaged face from her shoulder and stared at her with a burning intensity. 'Surely love like ours wasn't meant to be wasted,' he muttered, then sat up straight and pushed her back down amongst the pillows.

'I have to go and pack. The plane leaves at eleven. Jack will pick me up at the flat and drive me out. We'll say goodbye now, my darling. I couldn't bear to say goodbye in front of people and have to cry in front of them for more than just my father.'

She nodded, beyond words, as tears streamed down her cheeks and her throat closed over the knot which was lodged within it.

'I love you, Lucia,' he whispered, and pressed a kiss on her tear-wet lips.

She listened to his footsteps walk down the hall and across the veranda, even imagining that she could hear them on the steps, and then wrapped her arms around her shoulders and rocked back and forth, trying to stem the pain that racked her body.

Other footsteps on the veranda—deep voices, then a lighter one.

'I'm hallucinating,' she muttered to herself. 'That sounds like Mum.'

'Get up, Lucia!' her mother's voice cried and she leapt out of bed and flew across the room, sobbing as if her heart would break as she flung herself on her knees in the passageway and buried her face in her mother's lap.

'There, child, it's sad for your Matt but not the end
of everything.' Her mother was tugging at her hair
and she slid her fingers across her cheeks to wipe away
the tears and looked up blearily. Two of her brothers
stood behind her mother's chair and she frowned at
them. What were they doing away from the farm? Surely
they hadn't come just to lift her mother's chair up
the steps!

'What are you doing here?' she asked her mother
between pitiful sniffs and much blinking back of tears.
'Do you have to see the doctor?'

Tears threatened to flow afresh at the thought of 'her'
doctor but her mother shook her head.

'We've come to talk some sense to you and then, I
hope, to see you off,' her mother announced. 'Your aunt
phoned to tell us the bad news about your Matthieu and
then told us you would not stand beside him in his
trouble.'

Lucia blinked and shook her head, as if to clear away
the unbelievable idea her mother seemed to be voicing.

'I would stand by him in trouble, Mum,' she argued,
'if I could. But his trouble is in France! He has to
go home and he won't be able to come back for a
long time.'

Her voice wavered and broke, and she mumbled
things about mothers and sisters in a disjointed way that
even to herself sounded demented.

'If you love this man, even if his trouble is in
Timbuktu, then that is where you should be,' her mother
said sternly, and Lucia stared at this woman she thought
she knew in utter amazement.

'I can't go to France,' she stammered, and saw her
mother's frown grow fiercer.

'He doesn't want you with him? He doesn't love you enough to want your support at this time?'

'Of course he loves me,' Lucia cried, angry at the implied criticism of Matt. 'But he knows I wouldn't go—couldn't go, Mum. I couldn't go all that way and leave you.'

'Oh, Lucia!' her mother sighed. 'Haven't I told you that you must make your own life? Haven't I convinced you yet that I can manage without you? I will miss you, of course, because you are my beloved daughter and doubly dear because we had to grow strong again together, but you must seek your own destiny and go where love has chosen for you. France is not so very far from Italy, and hasn't your father always promised to take me there to see the village our ancestors left when they came to Australia?'

'But Matt's leaving today! At eleven!' Lucia cried, trying to stem a rising tide of excitement that was threatening to blot out any sanity.

'So, you can leave with him,' her mother said calmly. 'That's why the boys and your father have all come to town. To say goodbye to you.'

'My father, and the other two?'

Lucia's head spun but at that moment Aunt Steph appeared.

'Breakfast in the kitchen. I'll pack for you. You won't need much, apart from underwear and personal things, because you'll have to buy winter clothes when you get there.'

I should stop all this right now, Lucia thought, feeling as if she was being swept along on the crest of a wave that was escalating towards some unforeseen disaster. But she allowed one of her brothers to lead her into the kitchen and sit her at the table. Her mother dropped her passport, renewed last year when the family had taken a trip to New Zealand, in front of her.

'Your father rang the French Embassy in Canberra. Robert has the details of what must be done and he will take you to the French Consul and fix up the visa when you get to Brisbane.'

Lucia shook her head again. The world was spinning so quickly she wondered how she was clinging on.

'Robert?' she muttered, catching on to one familiar point of reference.

'Robert will go to Brisbane with you,' her mother said in a matter-of-fact way. 'After all, we don't want our daughter flying overseas without one of the family to see her off. And what would your young man think of it?'

I cannot imagine, Lucia thought, and for a fraction of a second she wondered if Matt would be dismayed if she let her family push her into his arms.

The question was answered before she drew another breath for Matt burst into the kitchen, followed at a more sober pace by her father and brothers, Michael and Robert.

Matt stopped by her side, then knelt and took her hand.

'Would you really come with me, my love?' he asked, his voice husky with hope and the grief in his eyes tempered by love.

'Would you like me to?' she whispered, running her fingers lightly over his face as if they could convey the messages of devotion bursting in her heart.

'Oh, Lucia, how can you ask that?' he murmured. 'I'll bring you back, if you're unhappy; let you go if you choose not to stay or if your heart misses your loved ones too much for you to be content. But if you could come, for a while at least, it would make the pain more bearable and fill so much of the loneliness in my heart.'

He pressed his head into her lap, as she had done to her mother only minutes earlier, and she looked up at the faces of those she loved so dearly and saw her tears reflected in their eyes.

'I'll come,' she whispered, tugging at his head so she could lean down and kiss him, sealing the pledge between them.

The remaining hours blurred into movement, as Lucia showered and changed. Her father drove her to the base and explained what was happening when she broke down and cried again in Leonie's arms.

'I'm really happy,' she sobbed, 'except for Matt, of course, and leaving you in the lurch like this, but you do understand I must go!'

'Of course you must,' Leonie agreed. 'Just keep in touch and remind that man of yours that we always need good eye specialists based here to visit places like Caltura.'

She pushed Lucia away and dried her eyes.

'We won't say goodbye yet,' she added. 'Jack decided we would leave Katie in charge and all slip out to the airport to wave you off. I know it will be a sad departure for both of you but you know that the best wishes of all of us, and the deep, abiding love of your family, will go with you.'

Lucia nodded, then breathed deeply.

It was time to stop crying. She had to be strong for both of them. She had to be the adventurer!

*   *   *

As the plane lifted into the sky above the bay, she held tightly to Matt's hand and watched the waving friends and family growing ever smaller.

'I love you, Lucia,' he whispered, and she knew everything was going to be all right.

The plane turned and banked, and Lucia watched the town disappear. Then beneath them, sun glinting off its wings, she saw a small, sleek RFDS plane lift and circle towards the hills, the wings dipped as if in salute to the mighty airliner.

'Look,' she said to Matt. 'Our last view of the Bay and there's one of our planes in it.'

'Allysha heading out to Cabbage Tree,' Matt said. 'I should have been on that flight.' He squeezed her hand, as if to reassure himself she was there, then said quietly, 'I wonder who'll they'll get to take my place?'

FREE

Return this coupon and we'll send you 4 Medical Romance™ novels and a mystery gift absolutely FREE! We'll even pay the postage and packing for you.

We're making you this offer to introduce you to the benefits of Reader Service: FREE home delivery of brand-new Medical Romance novels, at least a month before they are available in the shops, FREE gifts and a monthly Newsletter packed with information.

Accepting these FREE books and gift places you under no obligation to buy, you may cancel at any time, even after receiving just your free shipment. Simply complete the coupon below and send it to:

MILLS & BOON® READER SERVICE, FREEPOST, CROYDON, SURREY, CR9 3WZ.

No stamp needed

Yes, please send me 4 free Medical Romance novels and a mystery gift. I understand that unless you hear from me, I will receive 4 superb new titles every month for just £2.10* each, postage and packing free. I am under no obligation to purchase any books and I may cancel or suspend my subscription at any time, but the free books and gift will be mine to keep in any case. (I am over 18 years of age)

M6LE

Ms/Mrs/Miss/Mr _____

Address _____

_____

_____ Postcode _____

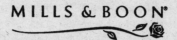

MILLS & BOON®

Medical Romance™

Books for enjoyment this month...

RESPONDING TO TREATMENT — Abigail Gordon
BRIDAL REMEDY — Marion Lennox
A WISH FOR CHRISTMAS — Josie Metcalfe
WINGS OF DUTY — Meredith Webber

Treats in store!

Watch next month for these absorbing stories...

TAKE A CHANCE ON LOVE — Jean Evans
PARTNERS IN LOVE — Maggie Kingsley
DRASTIC MEASURES — Laura MacDonald
PERFECT PARTNERS — Carol Wood